मुस्कुराती ज़िन्दगी

विकास तिवारी 'त्वष्टा'

कलम मेरी जब-जब उठती है
बग़ावत लिखती है।
क़िस्सा कुछ भी हो
हमे सिर्फ़ अदावत लिखती है।
शायद इसे भी उनसे इश्क़ हो गया
जब-जब उनका नाम आता है
उन्हें सिर्फ़ सलामत लिखती है ।।

सुबह कहूँ या शाम

बे-वजह हो तुम

लब पे लगा शराब कहूँ तो ख़राब हो तुम।

मैं जानता हूँ

मैं अच्छा नहीं हूँ

मगर मुझसे तो ख़राब हो तुम।

ख़ैर छोड़ो मेरी बात

बग़ैर मेरे

ख़ुद में ही बर्बाद हो तुम।

कई कमियाँ

कई खामियाँ है मुझमें

हो तुम शानदार

मगर बग़ैर मेरे

कहाँ मज़ेदार हो तुम।

कहीं और नहीं

किसी और में नहीं

अनजान होते हुए भी

मैं तुममें

मुझमें मुकम्मल हो तुम ॥

भरोसा ख़ुदा पर ख़ुद के लिए
ख़ुदा के खेल में रख
यहाँ हर पल तिलिस्मी बाज़ियाँ चलती है
आंधियाँ चलती है
फिर भी शम्मा जलती है।
रख थोड़ा धैर्य और
क्योंकि
समय से पहले तक़दीर भी कहाँ बदलती है ॥

रहने दो तनहा उन्हें
उनकी तनहाइयाँ उन्हें भाती है।
दुनिया के कोलाहल उन्हें बे-चैन करते है
अपनी तनहाइयों में वो ख़ुदको ढूँढ लेते है।
आफ़ताब तनहा है
महताब तनहा है
तनहा हर शक्स है यहाँ
क्योंकि
तनहाइयाँ मुकम्मल कर देती है।।

पिता के एहसासों को जाना
ज़िम्मेदारियों को जाना
मजबूरियों को जाना
हिस्सेदारियों को जाना
कमज़ोरियों को जाना।
पिता असमान है
जमीं है
होंठों की ख़ुशी है
आँखों की नमीं है।।

ये ज़िंदगी है
इसके मज़े बहुत है
और सजे?
बहुत है।
किरदारों की केंचुली
ओढ़ते छोड़ते दिन बीत जाएँगे।
हमारी पहचान मिलेगी
जाने किस किरदार में।
किस ओर है हम
सही, ग़लत या फिर हर ओर है हम।
कोई मक़सद है
या ग़ैर मक़सद है हम।
ज़िंदगी की लौ जल रही है
प्राणवायु अंदर बाहर चल रही है।
टूट जाता है पत्ता शाख़ से
मगर सफ़र ख़त्म नहीं होता।
ये सफ़र की इब्तिदा है
या सफ़र ख़त्म?

तुम सहर हो जाओ
अब शब अच्छी नहीं लगती
मैं वाक़िफ़ था तेरे जाने से
ये लौट आने की कोशिश अच्छी नहीं लगती ॥

सबके हिसाब से जीते-जीते
अपना हिसाब भूल गया।
वो नन्हा बालक कब स्कूल गया
कब घर का रास्ता भूल गया ।
वो माँ के हाथ का ख़ाना
वो माँ की लोरी सुनकर सोना
अब रातों में सुकून से सोना भूल गया।
सबके हिसाब से जीते-जीते
अपना हिसाब भूल गया।
बोझ उठाया उसने
कभी किताबों का
कभी सपनों का
कभी अपनों का
बस अपना उठाना भूल गया।
सबके हिसाब से जीते-जीते
अपना हिसाब भूल गया ।।

ये इम्तिहान की घड़ी है, तुम्हें पार होना है
तुम्हें साहिल में बैठना नहीं, न निराश होना है
तुम तो सिकंदर हो ज़िंदगी के तुम्हारे
समंदर में कूद जाओ, तुम्हें तैर के पार होना है ॥

यूँ भी एक दिन होगा
मुकम्मल हर अश्क़ होगा ।।

साहिल पर रहकर समंदर को निहारना
मौजों में रहकर लहरों से खेलना
मज़ा है दोनों में
मगर मुख़्तसर।
मुलाक़ात हुई उनसे
इश्क़ हुया उनसे
मज़ा है दोनों में
मगर मुख़्तसर ॥

ख़ुदा को झुक कर सलाम किया करो
इश्क़ करो
तो किसी को बदनाम किया करो ॥

कश्ती को डूबने का डर नहीं है।
डर है तो
सिर्फ़ किनारे लगने का ॥

टूटते तारे है
दुआ किसी की पूरी होती है।
दिल किसी के मिलते है
बात किसी की पूरी होती है ॥

समंदर में असंख्य लहरें उठती है
सबको साहिल हासिल नहीं होती।
टूट जाते है सितारे भी आसमान से
हर सितारे को ज़मीन हासिल नहीं होती।
हम इंसानों की हज़ार ख्वाहिशें है
हर ख्वाहिश को हक़ीक़त हासिल नहीं होती।
वक़्त, इश्क़, साँस और तक़दीर भी धोखा देती है
हर बशर को मुकम्मल ज़िंदगी हासिल नहीं होती ।।

एक बेचैनी है
जिसने जिगर में घर कर रखा है
मुझे मेरे ही घर से बेघर कर रखा है।
दिन तो कट जाता है बड़े एहतियात से
मुझे उसकी एक शब-ए- मुलाक़ात ने बड़ा बे-सबर कर रखा है।
मैं ज़िंदगी की राह में चलता चला जा रहा हूँ
ठहरना अब मुझे आता नहीं
ऐसा लगता है उसने मुझे अपना हमसफ़र कर रखा है।
ये तो उसके चहरे का नूर है
मुझे उसके साथ होते हुए
चाँद की ज़रूरत नहीं होती
शायद उसने खुदको मेरा नूर-ए -अजल कर रखा है।
हर कोई यहाँ मतलब से है
तू मेरे मतलब से है
या मैं तेरे मतलब से हूँ
शायद मोहब्बत ने हर किसी को मतलब का कर रखा है ॥

ख़ुशियाँ सबको खोज लेती हैं
ख़ैर छोड़ो
ख़ुशियाँ कौन चाहता है
हम तो दौड़ में है
हमे प्रथम आना है ॥

खिलते है जहां में फूल भी काँटे भी
हर कोई बस वक़्त पे काम आया है ॥

हम अपनी-अपनी तकलीफ़ों के बीज बोते है
भर संसार में सुना सुनाकर रोते है
हम तन्हा होते है, साथी तलाशते है
साथी के संग ग़म की गठरी खोलते है।।

यूँ बल्खा के चलती हो
मीलो मील चलती हो
ना थकती हो ना ठहरती हो
मौसमों का रुख़ लेती हो
मोड़ आते है कई सफ़र में
कुछ सोचकर
फिर निकल पड़ती हो
रुकती नहीं ख़ुद
बस ख़ुदा की हैरत को देखती हो
शायद तभी कभी सूखती हो
अपना रास्ता बनाये रखती हो
कई बार रास्तों के पार निकल पड़ती हो
तुम सृजन हो या सृजनकर्ता का मन
कितने ही निर्भर है तुम पर
कितने तुमसे खेलते है
कितनो का सबकुछ तुम हो
कितनो का सबकुछ छीन लेती हो तुम
जब क्रोध में होती हो
गाँव बसे खलिहान बने
शहर बसे फिर रेगिस्तान बने
तुमने समय देखा समय को बदलते देखा
तुमने समंदर देखा
कभी पूरा देखा
कभी अधूरा सफ़र देखा ॥

ये दुनिया जो तुम देख रहे हो
ये नहीं है।
ये शून्य है भावना से
लिप्त है काम भावना से
मतलब पूरा हो
फिर तुम कौन हम कौन
रिश्ते ज्यादा है वहाँ
जहां हर मतलब पूरा हो
मेरी हर भावना से
अल्प संभावना से नहीं,
ये दुनिया काग़ज़ी है
यहाँ फूल खिलते नहीं
मुरझाते नहीं
कुम्हलाते नहीं
बस एक रंग से रहते है
बड़ी पक्की संभावना से
तुम और मैं कौन है
बस कुछ किरदार
हम कुछ पल और चलेंगे
अपनी अपनी सम-विसम भावना से
हर तरफ़ मैं एक ही भाव देखता हूँ
या यूँ कहिए की हर चेहरे पर एक ही भावना चिपकी रहती है
खुदको छलते रहने की, औरों को छलते रहने की
मुस्कान इनकी सच नहीं है
रोना इनका सच नहीं है
हर दिशा में प्यार की नुमाइश है
हर पल प्यार की आज़माइश है
आप भाव में है तो पापी है
भावुक लोग यहाँ बड़ी भावना से ठगे जाते है
कहूँ किसे कि वो भावुक है
हो सकता है वो भी किसी को ठग रहा हो
फूल खिलते नहीं आज की दुनिया में
ना कुम्हलाते है

ना ही मुरझाते है
सदा खिले रहते है
सदा के लिए
इस काग़ज़ी दुनिया में ।।

टूटना काश उतना ही आसान होता
जितना की एक काँच का
काश मैं भी टूट जाऊँ
और वजूद ख़त्म हो जाये
मैं क्या ही कर रहा इस जहां में
कुछ खनिजों का हनन कर रहा हूँ
अपने बचे रहने के लिए
मेरा वजूद मुझसे सवाल करता है
मेरा होना या ना होना कोई मतलब है
मैं नहीं रहूँगा तो भी ये जहां ऐसा ही चलता रहेगा
कुछ पल के लिये शायद कुछ लोग संताप करेंगे
फिर उनकी ज़िंदगियाँ स्थिर हो जाएगी
मेरा वजूद या मेरा अहम
क्या है वो
जो मुझसे ये सवाल करता है
ग़र मैं टूट जाऊँ अभी तो कुछ परिवर्तन होगा इस जहां में
मुझे नहीं लगता की कुछ भी बदलेगा
बदलेगा?
मगर क्यों?
ग़र बदलेगा
तो वो भी कुछ वक़्त के ख़ातिर
उसके बाद फिर इस जहान में स्थिरता होगी
मेरा मुकम्मल कल नहीं आयेगा
उसकी कोई संभावना नहीं है ॥

गिरना तो तय है
तय तुम्हें करना है
गिरे रहना है
गिरने की हिम्मत करना है
गिर के उठने कि हिम्मत करना है
गिर के फिर गिरने का हौसला ना कम करना है
तय तुम्हें करना है
निर्णय जो भी लोगे
हर बार कुछ हानि कुछ लाभ होगा
मगर हर निर्णय में दोनों का ही अनुपात होगा
तय तुम्हें करना है
कुछ में हानि आज की होगी
कुछ में लाभ आज का होगा
कुछ में बहुत रोना आज होगा
कुछ में बहुत हँसना आज होगा
तय का ठीकरा सदैव तुम्हारे साथ होगा
तय तुम्हें करना है
कुछ तुम्हें मजबूरी में करने होंगे
कुछ मंज़ूरी में करने होंगे
मगर
करने ना -करने का
जिम्मा तुम्हारा अपना होगा
तय तुम्हें करना होगा
तय तुम्हें करना है ॥

जब-जब मैं मुड़कर देखता हूँ
आँखों से आंसू ढुलक आते है
अतीत की यादें
मेरी कमज़ोरियाँ
या कहूँ मेरे वक़्त का कमजोर होना,
मुझे एहसास दिलाता है
मैंने क्या किया है
मेरा करना सही था
जो मैंने किया है
या वक़्त अभी और वक़्त लेगा मुझे यक़ीन दिलाने में
मुझे सही या ग़लत बताने में
या सही ग़लत के फेर से निकालने में,
वक़्त बीत रहा है
मेरे एहसास शायद शून्य हो जाएँगे
इस बितते वक़्त में
शायद तब मुझे एहसास हो जाएगा
जो छूटना था वही वही छूटा है,
मैं मेरा तब भी था अब भी हूँ
कल रहूँ ना रहूँ
यादें बीते कल की
मेरे वर्तमान में अपनी अच्छी बुरी ख़ुशबू बिखेर देते है,
आज वही यादें मुझे एहसास दिलाते है
मेरे ज़िंदा रहने की
मेरे ना ना-उम्मीद होने की,
हर वक़्त बीत जाता है
थोड़ा वक़्त से हार के
थोड़ा वक़्त से जीत के ॥

खर्च कर दूँ मैं खुदको तुझपे

वजह ज़ाहिर तो होने दे।

ख़ुदा बना दूँ मैं तुझको

इबादत की वजह ज़ाहिर तो होने दे।

सुबह की रानाई कहूँगा तुझको

शब को तेरे संग गुजरने तो दे।

संग चलने का वादा करूँगा

दो कदम संग चलने तो दे।

ठंड में पश्मीना बन जाऊँगा तेरे ख़ातिर

थोड़ी ठंड तुझे लगने तो दे।

हर वजह साफ़ नज़र आये

मेरे साथ तुझे

ये ज़ाहिर होगा

ग़ैर ज़रूरी बातों को

हमारे बीच से पिघलने तो दे।

ख़ुदा ख़ुद आएगा हममें बसने के लिये

कुछ अहसास ख़ुदा को भी होने तो दे।

हमारी इश्क़- ए-ज़िंदगी लंबी नहीं मगर छोटी भी नहीं

दूरियों के दरिया को बहने तो दे।

मुकम्मल हम है या हमारा इश्क़

क्या मालूम

हमारे इश्क़ की बुनियाद जमने तो दे।

ये तो सदियों की बनाई कसौटी है

इसपे हमारे इश्क़ को खरा उतरने तो दे।

दूरियाँ हमारे बीच है

तू जानती है

मैं जानता हूँ

दुनिया को हमारी नजदीकियाँ समझने तो दे।

कागज की नाव पे हम हमारे इश्क़ को पार करेंगे

किसी तूफ़ान को दरिया-ए-इश्क़ पे उतरने तो दे ॥

कमियाँ कमाल की होती हैं
आँखों में नमियाँ कमाल की होती है
आपने याद आते है
जब दुनिया सवाल सी होती है ।।

प्रेम जब-जब अनंत हुया
प्रेम में रोम-रोम संत हुया।
राम ही मन राम ही देह
राम ही धरती राम ही व्योम हुया।
सुख गये मेरे हृदय में
राम ही बसंत हुया।
आदि से अंत तक चला
मिला तो सिर्फ़ राम ही अनंत हुया ।।

रौनक़ें

आज़ादियाँ

भरे पैमाने जाम से

चाहिए सबको आराम से।

आदमी को तौबा है काम से।

जानता है

मगर

शायद समझता नहीं

नहीं मिलता यहाँ कुछ भी आराम से।

मिलता है तो बस राम से, नाम से, काम से ॥

किरदार अकेला रहता है
किरदार मेरा ये कहता है
तू सबके दिल में रहता है।
ये और बात है
ग़लत सही के भेद में
तू अधूरा रहता है
किरदार अकेला रहता है।
चाँद सूरज धरा अगन सब कहते है
सच कहने पर तन्हा चलना पड़ता है
ग़लत सही के भेद में
किरदार अकेला रहता है।
मिट जाते है सब
एक-एक करके
मगर
मरकर भी
ग़लत सही के भेद में
किरदार अकेला रहता है ॥

किसी का ख़्वाब किसी की हक़ीक़त हो तुम
किसी की तबियत किसी कि ज़रूरत हो तुम
पंखों की उड़ान वो खुला आसमान हो तुम
मैं ही तुम हूँ, मेरी सिर्फ़ पहचान हो तुम ॥

एक कहानी है
एक लड़के के
वो लड़का है
या मर्द हो गया
क्या पता
मगर
वो विवाहित है।
उसे इश्क़ हुया
किसी ग़ैर से
अब वो पछता रहा ।।

कुसुम होना
मगर
कांटों से घिरे रहना
ये सिर्फ़ हिफ़ाज़त नहीं है
क़ीमत भी है तेरी ॥

मैं ग़लत हूँ
तू सही
तू स्वीकार तो कर
है इश्क़ दिल में तेरे
इज़हार कर
या
इंकार तो कर
लापता है वो परिंदा
जब उसने सुना
माशूक़ को उनसे इज़हार भी है
इनकार भी है ।।

खेला नहीं तो जाना क्या
ज़िंदगी के खेल में जीता क्या पाया क्या
मुहब्बत जीती या नफ़रत पायी
इस खेल में खुदको लगाया नहीं तो लगाया क्या?

आसमान खुला है
तुम उछलकर चूम लो इसे
इसे हैरानी होगी
ऐतराज़ नहीं ।।

माटी का खिलौना हूँ
अपना करतब दिखलाता हूँ
अच्छे बुरे का निर्णय तुम करो
चुपके से मैं जाता हूँ ।।

पिरोकर सबर के धागे में रिश्ते रखती है
माँ सबर का खजाना रखती है।
छोड़कर घर अपना किसी ग़ैर के पीछे आती है
पिता का घर छोड़ पति का घर सजाती है
माँ सबर का ख़ज़ाना रखती है।
कभी पति कभी सास कभी ननद का सुनती है
अपना दुख कहाँ किसी से कहती है
बिना कुछ कहे सौ दुख सहती है
माँ सबर का ख़ज़ाना रखती है।
रखकर नौ माह गर्भ में मुझे सब दर्द सहती है
जनकर मुझे मेरे चेहरे पे अपनी मुस्कान रखती है।
माँ सबर का ख़ज़ाना रखती है ॥

(सबर = सब्र)

कितना रंज पालोगे 'त्वष्टा'
किसी को तो छोड़ दो
मईयत उठाने वाले ना सही
कफ़न डालने वाले तो छोड़ दो।
कितने रास्ते तुम तक आते थे
तुमने सब मोड़ दिये।
वो कहते है बड़े तन्हा है
हमने कहा इश्क़ कर लीजिए
तन्हाई भाने लगेगी।
हमे ये ग़ुरूर हुया
जमाने में सिर्फ़ हम है
हमारा ग़ुरूर टूटा तो जाना
यहाँ मुनव्वर और भी है।
ये हमारे जमाने कि ख़ूबसूरती है
यहाँ इंसान कई है
इंसान की क़ीमत कुछ नहीं।
यहाँ दिल लगाने को कई चेहरे है
मगर यक़ीन के लिए एक भी नहीं।
वो कहते थे वो हमारे लिए शम्मा है
हमने हल्की सी हवा क्या दी
वो तो बुझ गये।
यहाँ हर कोई आशिक़ है
इश्क़, इश्क़ ना हुया
अंग्रेज़ी शराब हो गया
हर कोई डूब जाता है इसमें।
हम उनके लिए अनजान हो गये
जिनकी सुबह की पहली अजान थे।
अब तो टूटने से ख़ौफ़ नहीं होता
हम तो जापानी तरीक़े से जोड़े गए है
पहले से बेहद खूबसूरत और पाक हो गये है।
वो इश्क़ ही क्या इश्क़ हुया
जो आशिक़ ना बनाये
टूट जाने पर एहसास-ए-दर्द ना हो

छूट कर कविराज ना बनाये।
उन्हें भी एहसास-ए-इश्क़ हुया
जब हम उकता गए।
हर कोई क़ैदी है यहाँ
और वो सोचते है वो आज़ाद है।
हमे दादी नानी बचपन में कहानियाँ सुनाती थी भूपतियों के
आज हर कोई अपने किस्से सुना रहा।
जरा संभल के चलिए आप सितारे है
यहाँ सितारों के टूटने से लोग दुआयें माँगते है।
वो जो कभी हमसफ़र हमराह हमक़दम थे
आज अलग है।
वो हमारी सबसे अच्छी दुआ है
आज सोचते है काश ना की होती।
जमाने में ग़म बहुत है
शराब से इश्क़ करा दे ऐसा सिर्फ़ एक है।
उन्हें लगता है उनका अहम सदा के लिए है
धरा की गोद में जाने कितने अहम कब के सो चुके है।।

सब खेल तो उस स्रष्टा का है
रच कर दुनिया को
ख़ुद दुनिया हो गया
मिट्टी है
वायु है
आकाश है
जल है
अग्नि है
ध्वनि है
खुदको हर हिस्से में रखकर
हर हिस्से को हर पल भोगता
स्रष्टा अपनी दुनिया में है भी और नहीं भी
ग़लत सही
रात दिन
ऊपर नीचे
इधर उधर
यहाँ वहाँ
कोई वजह है या बे-वजह है
ये स्रष्टा सबकुछ है भी और नहीं भी
हर पल मरता
हर पल नया जन्म लेता है
दर्द भी है और ख़ुशी भी
सुख भी है दुख भी
इंसान है या जानवर भी नहीं
मै कहूँ ग़र वो इस पल यहीं है
तो मैं ग़लत हो सकता हूँ
सच यही है की वो है
हर पल में हर ज़र्रे में ॥

इस मै का ही तो सब खेल है

मुझमें और तुझमें इस मै का ही अंतर है बाक़ी सब एक है

ये मै अहम का प्रत्यक्ष रूप है

ये मै ही हर बंधन का श्रौत है

मै यहाँ, मै वहाँ

मै ये, मै वो

मै ऐसा, मै वैसा

कौन है मुझ जैसा

मै सबकुछ हूँ

मुझमें सब है

मै अधिकारों की बात करता हूँ

मै शक्ति की बात करता हूँ

मै कमजोरी को नकार देता हूँ

मै अपने अस्तित्व की हर पल पहचान कराता हूँ

मै विध्वंश हूँ

मै सृजन हूँ ॥

है कर्षण ऐसा मुझमें
बंधना तुम चाहो
बांध मैं लूँगा।
एहसास होगा नहीं
की तुम बंधन में हो ॥

हम सभी को बस एक उम्र गुज़ारनी है यहाँ।
उसमे भी इतना हंगामा हो जाता है ॥

तुम्हारे ज़िक्र से लबों पे मिठास होती है
फूल हो तुम
तुम्हारे होने से
मेरे आसपास महक होती है।
ज़िक्र सुनकर तुम्हारा
अब तो ग़ैरों से मोहब्बत होती है।
धड़कन मद्धम होती है
और
आँखों में चमक होती है।
वो जो आदतें मेरी
ऐब लगती थी तुम्हें
सब बदल गई है
अब तो बस मुझमें सिर्फ़ तुम्हारी आदतें होती है।
वो सुबहें
वो शामें
अब कहाँ?
अब कहाँ वो मुलाक़ातें होती है
अब तो सिर्फ़ यादें है
उन यादों की तह में सिर्फ़ बीते वक़्त कि चहक होती है।
आगे अभी सफ़र और है
तुम्हारे भी
मेरे भी
ये इब्तिदा- ए- सफ़र था जो मिल गये
मिलना नसीब था
बिछड़ना हक़ीक़त है
फिर से मिलने की बस ललक होती है ।।

ये मेरी इब्तिदा है
ईतेहाँ का
इंतज़ार करो
खबर होगी तुम्हें मेरी जीत कि
जरा खुदको बेक़रार करो
आपने मेरी मोहब्बत देखी है
परवाह निगाहें दिखीं है
मेरे एहतराम का मज़ा लिया है
मेरे ऐतराज़ पर ना अब तुम इनकार करो
मेरे कीर्ति का अब ये सूरज नहीं ढलेगा
इसका एहसास तुम बेशुमार करो ।।

कितना कुछ है कहने को
कह नहीं सकते।
वो सुन तो सकते है
समझ नहीं सकते
इंतज़ार
हम करना चाहें भी
मगर कर नहीं सकते।
वो मेरे है
वो मेरे हो नहीं सकते।
एक अजब सी दुनिया में रहते है
कि
हम किसी की चाहत है
हम किसी को चाहते है
हम उन्हें नहीं मिलते जो हमे चाहतें है
हम मिलते है उन्हें
जो हमे नहीं
किसी और को चाहतें है।
हम जी तो सकते है
इस जीने को समझ नहीं सकते ॥

ये किसने मेरी तन्हाई को भंग किया
ये किसने मेरी खामोशी में कोलाहल घोल दिया।
आँख खुली तो तुमको देखा
और तुमने
बस बाबा ही बोल दिया।
दिन बदले दुनिया बदली
नन्ही सी तुमने जनम लिया
एहसासों की शून्य धरा में
बस एहसासों को घोल दिया ।।

हिम्मत करके
पहला कदम बढ़ाना
और हार जाना।
प्रारब्ध से लड़ना
और
टूट जाना।
हवा के झोंके बड़े जोर के थे
उस परिंदे ने
घरौंदा बनाया
तिनकों का सहारा लेकर
हवा के झोंके ने
घरौंदा उड़ाया।
परिंदे को किसी ने बताया नहीं
चुप से हार जाना।
तुम भी बिखर गये हो
सिमट कर फिर कदम बढ़ाओ
फिर हिम्मत कर कदम उठाओ।
घरौंदा बना है उसी डाली पर
नन्हे चूज़ों से सजा है उसी डाली पर
अब तो शायद शजर गिर जाये
कोई हवा उड़ा नहीं सकती उस घरौंदे को।
तुमने अपने सपने को हक़ीक़त कर लिया है
अब तो तुमने भी प्रारब्ध पर फ़तह किया है
बिखर कर सिमटना सीख लिया है
तुमने भी हार के जीतना सीख लिया है।।

वो मुक़द्दस तक़दीर लाये है।
तारे जमीं पर खींच लाये है।
हम यहाँ रोटियों के बिना सोते है।
वो अपने दर्द भी शीशे पर उतार लाये है ।।

आदतें मेरी,
उसकी
अलग नहीं है।
करके मुहब्बत भूल जाता हूँ
पल भर पहले किया वादा
निभाना भूल जाता हूँ
पकड़ ली सांस की डोरी उसने मेरी,
दौड़ कर दूर जाता हूँ, हर बार लौट आता हूँ
मैं उससे दामन छुड़ाना भूल जाता हूँ।
वो ठहरी समंदर सी है
मैं भाप बनकर छूट जाता हूँ
करके यात्रा जहां भर की
बनकर बूँद फिर उसी में लौट आता हूँ
मैं उससे दामन छुड़ाना भूल जाता हूँ।।

तुमसे रंज भी है , मोहब्बत भी
निभाते है दोनों ही, रह रह कर ॥

तुम भी बेवक़ूफ़ियाँ कर सकते हो।
हर बार समझदारी ज़रूरी नहीं ।।

लोकतंत्र में सच और झूठ नहीं होता,
होता है
तो सिर्फ़ बहुमत ।।

मुख़्तसर ज़िंदगी में ये मुलाक़ात मुख़्तसर है
इस मुख़्तसर मुलाक़ात को मुख़्तसर रहने दो ॥

अपने होने के सबूत छोड़ गया वो

अपने होने के सबूत छोड़ गया वो
ज़िंदा था
शायद मर गया वो।
कहता था भुला दूँगा दुनिया को
भूल जाएगी दुनिया मुझे
हँसकर गया वो
दुनिया को रुला गया वो।
हम सब सिमटने की बात कहते थे
बिखरना ज़िंदगी है कहता था वो
कहना नहीं की मर गया वो
कह देना सकुशल बिखर गया वो।
एक फूल जब तक महक रखता है
उसके आसपास रौनक़ महकती है
वो जो ज़िंदा था
हमारे आसपास उसकी चहल क़दमी महकती थी
अपने होने के सबूत छोड़ गया वो
ज़िंदा था
शायद मर गया वो ॥

एक ज़िंदगी मिली थी डू इट योरसेल्फ प्रोजेक्ट की तरह।
हमने आधी जी ली स्कूल कॉलेज के प्रोजेक्ट की तरह॥

मुकम्मल अश्क़ आखों से उतर गये
अशिक़ी धरी की धरी रह गई।।

ज़िक्र-ए-उल्फ़त में रह गये थे
जवानी के दिन मोहब्बत में बह गये थे।
सिर्फ़ दरवाज़ा बचा था, बुढ़ापे ने उस पर दस्तक दी
नींद खुली तो देखा बचे तो सिर्फ़ हम और वो दरवाज़ा
बाक़ी सब बह गये थे।।

हर ज़िंदगी का निचोड़ है यहाँ
एक कहानी!
जो अब कोई सुनता नहीं
कोई सुनता है मगर समझता नहीं
जो समझ गये
वो अपनी ज़िंदगी में बदलाव नहीं करते।
और फिर वही कहानी
बस चरित्र बदल कर कहते है।

इस जगत में हर वो जर्रा जहां है
उसकी वजह है, वो जहां है।
ढूँढते क्यों हो तुम खुदको?
ख़ुद ख़ुदा ने बनाया है तुम्हें
और वो जानता है तू कहाँ है ।
फूल खिलने से पहले वजह नहीं पूछता
शाख़ों पर कोपलें नयी निकल आती है।

उन्होंने मुसलसल रोका ही मुझे
इश्क़ की दीवार फाँदते हुए पकड़ा
और टोका ही मुझे।
ख़ैर उनका अपना तजुर्बा था
मेरी अपनी जवानी थी,
मैं जो जी रहा था आज
कभी वो उनकी कहानी थी।

वो जो दिखता नहीं
सबको उसी की तलाश है।
दीद होती नहीं उस सूरत की
और उसी सूरत की प्यास है।
ईश्वर है कि प्रेम है या मोह की माया है
ये भ्रम दूर है, कि आसपास है।
सब ग्रंथों का निचोड़ है,
ये दुनिया मिथ्या है
और सिर्फ़ प्यास है।
ये अजायबघर है
की जंगल है,
नियम एक सा नहीं
यहाँ सिर्फ़ नियमों का एहसास है।
रच के जहां को
रचनाकार जहां हो गया
लगता है,कभी दूर है कभी पास है ।।

हमारा इश्क़ एकतरफ़ा हुया तो क्या हुया
हमे दाग मख़मली मिला
हम टूट गये और बिखर गये
हम हिना के रंग से निखर गये
सौ वादों में एक वादा ना निभाया उसने
हम भी अपने हर वादे से मुकर गये।।
हमारा इश्क़ एकतरफ़ा हुया तो क्या हुया
हमे दाग़ मख़मली मिला
वो दिन याद किया करते होंगे वो
हमे बहुत याद किया करते होंगे वो
जब बात नहीं कर सकते तो
क्या ख़ाक याद किया करते होंगे वो।।
हमारा इश्क़ एकतरफ़ा हुया तो क्या हुया
हमे दाग़ मख़मली मिला
हमे उनकी हरारत का एहसास हुया
हमे उनकी हर शरारत का एहसास हुया
वो ठहरे नहीं मुड़कर देखा नहीं
जब उन्हें हमारी शरारत का एहसास हुया।।
हमारा इश्क़ एकतरफ़ा हुया तो क्या हुया
हमे दाग़ मख़मली मिला
यूँ अजनबी हो गये कि कभी मिले ही नहीं
यूँ मुरझा गए कि कभी खिले ही नहीं
यूँ भी एक रोज़ मुलाक़ात होगी
फिर एहसास होगा कि इस शक्स से कभी मिले ही नहीं।।
हमारा इश्क़ एकतरफ़ा हुया तो क्या हुया
हमे दाग़ मख़मली मिले
वो दोनों ही एक दूजे के इश्क़ में है
एहसास नहीं कि एक दूजे के इश्क़ में है
ये इश्क़ एकतरफ़ा हुया तो क्या हुया
वो आज भी एक दूजे के इश्क़ में है।।
हमारा इश्क़ एकतरफ़ा हुया तो क्या हुया
हमे दाग़ मख़मली मिले

सब अपने-अपने हिस्से के रहे
जो भी,
जितना रहे मेरे किस्से के हिस्से रहे।
कुछ उठकर चल दिये,
कुछ साथ बैठे रहे
मैं समझा यही मेरे हिस्से के रहे।।

समंदर में डूब जाना बुरा नहीं है।
बुरा होगा
समंदर में उतरने का साहस ना कर पाना।
टूट जाएँगे हम सफ़र में
शायद,
मिल नहीं पायेंगे हम खुदसे
गर सफ़र में चलने का संकल्प ना कर पाये।
बुरा कुछ भी नहीं है,
बुरा है क्रियाहीन होना।
बुरा है आत्महीन होना ॥

शाख़ों पे पत्ते जो लगे हैं
एक दिन टूट जाएँगे।
शाख़ों से छूटकर
ज़मीन पर बिखर जाएँगे।
गम किसका करते हो,
जो तुम्हारे है
साथ जाएँगे
जो ग़ैर है
तुम्हें छोड़ जाएँगे।
समंदर को बुंदों ने छोड़ा
फूलों ने वृक्षों को
ना समंदर ने ग़म किया ना वृक्षों ने।
छूटना व टूटना नियति का अनुबंध है
टूटकर छूटते है
छूटकर बनते है।
ग़म किसका करते हो,
जो तुम्हारे है
साथ जाएँगे
जो ग़ैर है
तुम्हें छोड़ जाएँगे ॥

किसी का होना, किसी से बिछड़ जाना
समंदर से छूटकर मल्हार हो जाना, बूँदों का निर्णय नहीं प्रारब्ध है॥

हमारी कमियाँ भी ग़ज़ब का खेल खेलती हैं
किसी को दूर रखती है किसी को नज़दीक रखती हैं।
वो जो हर कमियों को पार रखता है
ज़िंदगी भी उन्हीं पर हमारे हमसफ़र का पद भार रखती हैं।
बदलते समय पर हम भी बदलते हैं
और बदलती हैं कमियाँ
जो इन कमियों को दरकिनार रखते हैं
ज़िंदगी भी उन पर एतबार रखती है।
सिसक कर टूट जाती है कमियाँ
जो सब्र का समंदर रखते है,
अंत आते-आते दो एक हो जाते है
और उन्हीं पर साथ-ए-अंत का दारोमदार रखती है ।।

मैं गलत हूँ
स्वीकार करता हूँ
जो सही है
उनके साथ तो वफादारी निभाइये।
आपने कहा मैं कमज़ोर हूँ
मैंने स्वीकार किया
जो मजबूत है उनका बल बनिये।
आपने कहा मैं बे-औकात हूँ
मेरी सृजन मेरी औकात न बता सका
मैं स्वीकार करता हूँ
जिन्हे उनकी औकात पता है
उनकी औकात मे जीकर देखिये।
मैंने माना मैं सर्व गुणों से निर्गुण हूँ
सगुणों के सगुणों को आप स्वीकार तो करिये।
मेरी कमियाँ निहारि है आपने
मेरी खूबियों को नजरंदाज किया है आपने
किसी की कमियों को नजरंदाज करके
किसी की खूबियों को निहारिये।
हर पल जिंदगी मे गम हो
हर पल जिंदगी श्वेत कागज की तरह बेदाग हो
हर पल जिंदगी दिये की लौ सी जगमग हो
हर कोई हर पल आपके हर ख्वाब हर जज्बात को समझे
अच्छी बात है
हम ना समझ सके
हम स्वीकार करते हैं
जो आपको दिया हर वादा निभाए
उनसे एक वादा निभाइये।
जिंदगी आवाज की ध्वनि तरंगों सी है
जिसमें दुःखों की खाई है तो सुख की ऊँचाई भी है
इस बात को आप भी एक बार स्विकारिये।।

कभी किसी को बिना
वजह प्यार करके देखो…
उसकी खूबियों से नही
कमियों से प्यार करके देखो…
उसकी सूरत से नही
सीरत से प्यार करके देखो…
जिसे चाहने लगे हो
कभी उसका आईना बनके देखो….
भरोसा गर वो तोड़े कई बार
तो एक और बार भरोसा करके देखो…
गर कभी बेवफा हो जाये वो तो
एक बार उसकी आँखों मे उतर कर देखो…

कुछ दिनों से देख रहा हूँ।
एक लड़की है,जो कुछ कहती तो नही
मगर मेरे आसपास रहती है।
हमारी आंखे कई बार मिलती है
उसकी चोरी मैं पकड़ लेता हूँ।
मगर वो दूर रहती है
कुछ कहती नही है।
मैं तो बेमतलब सा
इन सब के बारे में।
मैं कोई अच्छा नही
शायद इसीलिए
मैं खुद को उससे बात
करने के लिए उकसाता नही।
वो दूर है कुछ कहती नही।
अच्छा है शायद कुछ कहती नही।।

मेरे अल्फ़ाज़ लड़खड़ाए
जब वो नज़र आए।
तुष्टि तो उसे पा के भी ना होगी
बस दूर से देख उसे
मेरी रूह सुकून पाए।
उसकी चमकती आंखें
और उनसे वो बात करे
मेरी जाहिल आंखें
कहां उसकी बातें समझ पाए।
मुकम्मल में हो जाऊंगा
गर वो मुझे पाए,
मैं आशिकों की महफ़िल में शामिल
हो जाऊंगा
गर वो आशिकी निभाए।
शीशे सा है उसका बदन
मगर मेरी चाहत उसकी रूप की
मोहताज नहीं
मैं हर पल उसको चाहूंगा
चाहे वो कितने ही रूप बदलती जाए।।

सफर में हम सब है
कोई साथ चल दे तो बुरा क्या है।
कुछ वक़्त ही सही
वो साथ है तो
बुरा क्या है।
बरगद के पेड़ की छाया सा
महसूस वो हो तो बुरा क्या है।
गर प्यास में
कुंए के पानी सा गले को
तर कर दे तो बुरा क्या है।
सफर हमारा साथ है
शायद मंजिल तक नहीं
मगर कुछ पल साथ है तो बुरा क्या है।
कुछ गलतियां हुई
कुछ नादानियां
साथ में की
कुछ रोए
कुछ हंस लिए
साथ में तो बुरा क्या है।
सफर में कोई ख्याल करता
कोई वजह बन जाए
मुस्कुराहट की
तो बुरा क्या है।
तू सफर में है
ये याद है तुझको
सबसे बेखबर तो बुरा क्या है।।

जो करते है, वो बोलते नहीं उनका काम बोलता है
वो काम कर गए और मर गए,
और आज उनका नाम हर इंसान बोलता है।
चंद लम्हों की मेहनत नहीं, ये जिंदगी की कमाई है
पल-पल की खुशियां,उन्होंने घंटों की मेहनत मे गंवाई है।
ये इंसान नहीं, इंसान का काम बोलता है
छोटे-छोटे क़दमों से चले, गिरे फिर चल पड़े
हासिल किया वो मकाम
आज वो नहीं है मगर उनका वो मकाम बोलता है।
सच और मेहनत के साथ चलने वाली की मंजिल दूर होती है
मगर हासिल होती है
यह पैग़ाम मैं ही नहीं, दुनियां का हर परेशान इंसान बोलता है।
दंभ उनके भी टूटे, चोटें उनको भी लगी मगर मेहनत करते रहे
की आज इतिहास का हर पन्ना उनकी मेहनत का शक्सियत-ए-बखान बोलता है।

तेरी चरण धूलि मिली है
मिलेगा सबकुछ।
तेरा था बेटा तेरा ही रहूँगा
सुख संसार के सारे झूठे है।
तेरे चरणों में आके
न रही अब ख्वाहिश सुख की
तेरे दर्शन से प्रभु के दर्शन होते
अब ना रही ख्वाहिश किसी दर्शन की।
गम की चिंता क्या करूँ
चरणों में तेरे हर फ़िक्र है मेरी मिट गयी।
तुहि वैष्णवी तुहि रुद्राणी
तुहि दुर्गा अरु विकराली।
मानुष का जन्म दिया तूने
सत्य असत्य का पाठ दिया तूने
लाल बनाया मुझको खुदका
हरपाल साथ दिया तूने।
तेरे चरणों की धुल से बने ये धाम
क्या मतलब तुझे छोड़ जाऊं मैं धाम।
माँ तेरा आशीर्वाद रखना, सर पे मेरे तेरा हाथ रखना।
माँ तेरा गुणगान मैं क्या गाऊं
तू तो अनंत अविनाशी है।
बस माँ अपने लालों का हर पल ख्याल रखना
मेरे सर पे अपना हाथ रखना।।

रोने को गम कम नहीं है
आँखें बरस सकती है
फिर से समंदर भर सकती है
उसके इंतज़ार में
रोने को गम कम नहीं है।।
वो इश्क़ में था मेरे
मैं इश्क़ में था उसके
रुकने को वजहें बहुत है
जाने को एक ही बहुत है
रोने को गम कम नहीं है।।
किसी की ज़िंदगी में शामिल होकर जाना
साथ चलना क्या है
बिछड़ना एक मोड़ से
जाना ये जो वक़्त जिये संग
ज़िंदगी जीने को कम नहीं है
रोने को गम कम नहीं है।।
फिर से शुरू होगी ज़िंदगी
फिर से वही गलती होगी
फिर से वही परिणाम होंगे
रोने को वक़्त बहुत है
रोने को गम कम नहीं है ।।

My one lesson is I am weak
But I'm proud to be.

If Thoughts Could
Be More Haunting

If thoughts could ever be more haunting
A heart so cold deserves some warmth
Most beautiful
Most bright
The brightest light couldn't touch it
A heart never broken or even bent
Would break when cold touches it.

If thoughts could ever be more haunting
She'll cry but never out loud
She'll cut and not let it show
She misses the cold
There's hope for a heart so gone
Is there hope for a love so wrong?
She will struggle to survive.

If thoughts could ever be more haunting
A heart so cold, dreams of her
A heart so cold, still pulls away
He resents her
He hates because happiness is just a dream

He survives by hurting himself
His heart's too cold to bleed.

If thoughts could ever be more haunting
Then I hope they're not about you.

Shine Through Me

34

Everyone lives to leave
Forget everything
Cause no one leaves with me.

Alone we walk
And hear God weep
Loves a word that's lost all meaning.

His eyes see through that
They see through me
In darkness I lie
As it constantly surrounds me
There's a light begging to be seen.

Loves Runaway

Hold my hand today
I'll hate you tomorrow
You saw what happens to me
Now I'm making you leave
You pity me
You care for me
That's why you can't stay
Please don't get attached
Don't get too close
Don't look or understand me
I love easy
But leaving's easier
You're gonna do more than bleed
Please leave
'Cause you'll never understand me
I do love you today
Tomorrow I'll still be gone
I pity myself
I lack self-esteem
I hate myself
'Cause I love a man
That I'm going to leave.

Forgetting You

At night I pretend you don't exist
Hoping to get a moment's rest
I close my eyes and I'll drift to sleep
But of course, in my dreams you'd be
I'll never touch those lips again
Or feel your sweet embrace
I fight my tears and my love
For you, a man so far away
It's nightmares now
I wake up screaming
And awake I'll stay
'Cause the thought of you scares me
But all that's left is a name
Your face I am forgetting.

Only A Thought

The biggest monster beats inside your chest
A heart will beat once or twice
Will stop momentarily to hear the mind's thoughts
Hearing those words your heart makes haste
Bound in fear of this, that was never there.

Choose A Side

On which part of the shore do you lie
On the path of darkness
Dirt and grime
Where sinners dwell
And love never survives
There the demons pull you too
But no one hurts you but you.

On the path of light
Hopeful and blissful it seems
But the darkness soon comes everyone's way
You constantly push
You shove and fight
When there is no more hope
That's when the demons strike.

Love In Pain

It bursts
Blown to pieces
Yet it's never been more whole
To hurt
To break
To be broken
This is better than to never know love.

Painful
And the pain brings clarity
The tears remind me
My heart beats faster than my mind can think
I let myself love
Knowing I am nothing
And as my heart dies
My love flourishes
Every time they scar me.

Shadows

Surround me
And I remain
I grow as you rise
I fall when you sink.

Even though we're opposites
Without you my existence wouldn't be evident.

The brighter your light
The darker I become
Your light keeps me going
I see beauty in your art
You'll never notice me
Darkness will always be lonely.

Hate Makes the Heart Grow Fonder

Heavy is your breath in my ear
Your words weigh down my spirit
My love glows brighter
With every cynical move you make
Crush every aspect of me and my meaning
Drain the life from me
Slowly spill out everything
Take it away
Then I will love you until my heart stops beating.

In My Head

It's begging me
And I can't
God, he's begging me
And I'm scared
Calling me
And life can't let it be
He does these things
And once again I'm crazy
God, he's begging me
And you show no mercy.

Loving A Monster

Take me tonight so I may dream of the tomorrow
Hold my hand
Through the light parts
Of my dark reality
Take me away
So, no one can ever find me
I will lay with the
For eternity

Feed on my flesh
It barely cuts
But it's enough to sting
He begs for my screams
I will indulge his every whim.

That Old-Time Religion

God didn't abandon me
I abandoned him
But one slit to the wrist and I can feel heaven again
God was never words in a book
God was never a faith to believe
God's always been there for me
An invisible friend
Which is something I need
He was there when all of you abandoned me
I devote myself to him completely
'Cause God does love you
And his love embraces me
So, you can laugh and hate me for what I believe
Because without God
I would have been alone from the beginning.

Invisible

45

One heart
One dream
One life
Goes unseen
The pain goes deep
No one hears the screams
Suffocating in a world
With little to no meaning.

Pawns

Darkness covers your eyes
Because you're on the brighter side
Darkness looks at you
He's blinded by the light
Yet he sees your beauty.

Darkness and light
Forbidden to love
Forbidden to touch
They use us as pawns
They allow us to touch.

Darkness gives you hope
But with light you give up
For us to love is forbidden
Darkness and light
But we still touch.

The Evil

It all starts the same
You're born to love
And your love will gradually grow
Share this thought
This beauty with anyone
And with everyone
Because no one will tell you
They don't tell you of THE EVIL.

THE EVIL finds you
Then your soul is gone
The traits you were born with
Your will for life
Your one purpose is gone.

You still go on
Looking for hope
But now you
You, yourself are taking souls!

Cursed Love

My heart beats fast but my feet are cold
They long for something I cannot hold.

A love that is not mine
A heart in decline
Yet I still long for it
And his love is forfeit.

He's loved before
So, his heart is not whole
His heart was steady
But he wanted more.

Her love he couldn't trust
Her heart was not enough
He gained her affection
Then left her in the dust.

Alone

Pail
Thoughtless
Cold
Still I reside alone.

By my side
No one
And not one hand to hold.

I lie dying
I tremble
I'm weak.

I fear for a life
But it never belonged to me
Hold on, tomorrow, here I come.

I only go and find
Tomorrow is yesterday
Every day like the day before.

Has a life no one got
For ones' own everyone lives

And I myself am the same.

Forever alone will we all remain
Even dying
By ourselves we shall lay.

At Love's Cost

My heart flutters and flies
Love flows faster than any current
Deep… That's how I feel
As much as I love so must I hate
Animosity and resentment darken my heart
Love and hate tear me apart
Documenting everything
So, one day remorse and hate can consume me
I'm swallowed by what once was a good soul
The memories of those I once loved forever haunt me.

Life's A Struggle

Crawl under my skin
Through my veins
Out my wrist
Hurt me and feel
More than the unknown
I cry inside
It's dark and cold
Look to my head
As it spins around
Look to my chest
As beats are skipped.

I stumble for my footing
My knees give in on me
It's a struggle
Not one part of me wants to keep going.

Jacob

So bright
So beautiful
And so full of life.

As I raise you above the sky
Stars couldn't shine brighter
You replace the sun.

You create these feelings
In everyone
You are what life is meant to be
Keep shining
Keep being life
And I will shy behind.

I found someone worth following

Just One Kiss

Kiss me and forget
Everyone that made you bleed
Everything worth remembering
Kiss me and we'll leave
Every bad and good memory
Create a new world
Kiss me and I promise
All the pain is released through me
And the new pain will never be forgotten
Kiss me and I know
I can keep you alive
I can give you meaning
Kiss me
Before it's too late.

With Myself at The Cemetery

My heart's final beat was skipped
Death was too exciting to miss
Maggots and worms feed on my eyes
Behind them though is where the good things lie
My brain is sleeping
But for them a delicious feast
Burrowing holes into thoughts I didn't know exist
In my head is where they'd keep warm
For my skin grew cold
I'm a bag of rotting flesh
Still, I never thought myself beautiful
That was until all this
Hair falls out
You're growing bald
But why bother to grow
When your soul is gone
Beauty forgets
It doesn't want to know
You keep your beauty after your lips get cold
But beauty soon too will leave
The smell of death
It should be bottled and sold

Give it to everyone
Except the old
They reek of it
Even as they breathe
A smell so mesmerizing
Back in your coffin
Only a few things remain
They feed on you and you can do nothing
After I watch my body made into a feast
I love to watch the others scream in fear and agony.

In The Dark

A voice so faint
It's not even there
But in its whispers
Is my name
Too scared to sleep
'Cause I might see it there
Haunt my dreams
Or steal my soul
Whatever your intentions
I will prevent them.

But why not fall asleep and stay there
It might be lovely
It might even care
I think it has stolen me
But only my heart
Because I'm never alone in the dark
It is beautiful
It is kind
It may be a demon
But this demon is mine.

Trust In Someone True

When you're down
When you're weak
Look to me
Just look at me
I'll stop your pain
I'll be your feet
I'll go to any length
To put a smile on your face
My only purpose in life
Is to be here for you
So just look at me
When you're down
When you're weak
When you're scared
Or when you're in need
I was placed here for you
So, for once look at me
'Cause even when you don't
I can feel it
I feel your pain
I can see it in your eyes
As it streams down your face
I'll stand here by your side
I'm here for the rest of your life.

Faking A Reality

If hearts could be damaged
Mine would bleed
In every attempt I make to leave
A little piece of me leaves
I hurt when hurting people
Smile
Laugh
Hide the scars
Throw up the pills
Move from the edge
Keep damaging you and your soul
So no one else can see
Pretend to keep love and friends
Pretend to be happy so loneliness won't find me.

Mad Hatter Syndrome

My life is fake
I'm a puppet on a string
When you cut them, I'm just another toy
At a tea party
A baby doll for a little girl
Who controls my arms and feet
Where I go and what I eat
My thoughts don't even belong to me
This is reality
And the fate of everyone
A life that everyone leads.

Ever Ending

Someone save me
Save me from me
I don't know where I'm going
I'm scared of who I'll be.

Unsure of my surroundings
Life's not for me
It's full of hate and disease
People not like me.

Looking forward
Looking back
Then looking at this paper
Life's kicking my ass.

Doing what I can to stay close
Close to him and my past
Slit cut slash
To make the pain go away fast.

Like that I'm weak
And sleep for the rest of eternity
Goodbye, love
And daydreams.

Hollow Souls

A life with no soul
A heart with a hole
Her eyes were so cold
Such a lifeless girl.

Hopeless and drained
Empty and blood-stained
Clearly it's all red
But she's still more alive than dead.

She rules
She reigns
Causing chaos and pain
But she does so with beauty and grace.

Only once will she smile
In a world full of sorrow
Where she causes most of the pain
But his heart will never be the same.

Scarlet

Grace my lips with your sin
I long for our touch again
To feel a pain
Not so easily forgotten
You hurt me
But I lust for another
Just one more kiss.

Break me again
So I can feed you
In return
Quench my thirst
And touch my skin
Drape over me
With scarlet streams.

Fire Is Fire

Love hurts as much as hate
So let's strike a match
And ignite the flame.

Feed on innocence
Feed on faith
Let it feed on violence
Blood
And rape.

Because love can kill you
Just as sure as hate
Fire is fire
It all burns the same
And it doesn't discriminate.

Running Red

Darkness
It's all I can see
My heart's black
My love is strong
And my knees are weak
Bring me down
I'm lower than the dirt beneath your feet
My head spins
Gravity forgot about me
Water always looked black to me
Today it ran red
The colors were changing
I lied there
He came in
But it was too late
The water was clear
I never realized how clear water could be.

Loving The Wrong Way

I cry when he looks at me
With eyes that don't even exist
Feed into my delusions
As I look into a face that's empty
Seamlessly fake
A fraud
Whispers of false truths
A tongue like a snake
With a body like heaven
A black hole for a heart
And ice-cold hands
A man less than human
Yet I've known you no other way
You're why my heart breaks
And grows every day.

What I Feel

Pain isn't a feeling
It's a thought.

Depression isn't a disorder
It's pain.

Love isn't reality
It's a delusion.

Magic isn't fake
It's love.

Happiness isn't something to be had
It's something to be earned.

Respect isn't bad
It's happiness.

What I feel isn't life
It's death.

Death isn't real
So it's not what I feel.

Love Then Not

Love is too easy
But so hard
Love is so close
But so far
Love's here
Then gone
Loving some
Then none
Love me
And then her
Love thought we are
No, we were
Love's what we got
No love's what we're not.

In Response

I haven't been driving
I'm not even in the car
I jumped out before you turned to start
I'll keep your flowers
But please no more
You've given me a garden
My heart is torn
That someone is here
As you come and go
I would hold you
But you're never here to hold.

Lost

Feeling lost
Scared
You don't know where you are
Do you panic?
Are you confused?
Are you really lost?
Maybe it's not that you're lost
You're just afraid of what you found.

Empty

Never before has love had so little meaning
Your promises
Mean nothing
Your words
Are empty
My eyes grow dull
As my soul gradually leaves
But it was never truly there
In the beginning.

Forgotten Dreams

Follow the feathers
They lead to the sky
But the bird who left them was flightless
Floating in the sky the feathers stay
Someone's hopes and dreams for me to crush
I blew all the feathers away
They fell to the ground
Occasionally spinning in the dust
You chase after them
Like they were some kind of big deal
And you left me behind
Maybe the light was blinding
Or you just didn't realize
I was your last feather in the sky
I fall to the ground
Broken and shattered like glass
I did the impossible
I planted a seed
So that my love may always last
No wishes
No dreams
No hopes
I wiped out your soul

Black eyes
A dead life
My spirit still haunts you
But gently guides you
I still follow you to the depths of hell
Holding your hand
I eventually sprout
A beautiful tree
You finally get your wings
I extend my branch
There you'll stay with another woman
Not just some kid like me.

Drip, Drip, Drip

Painted on smiles
Color on the bathroom tiles
Dying underneath the face paint
Smeared more color, feeling faint.

Drown in color

Red, it tastes good
It feels good
Paint's smearing
Water and tearing
Washing it away.

Drip, drip, drip
A slight grin
Spilling more color
I fall down
Dead
On the bathroom ground.

Quick Quip

If love was a flower
It'd die
But you'd suffer
'Cause it dies slowly.

Persevere

My first and only step
I am not small, the step is big
I will fall over and over again
The ground will break my fall
The ground will catch me
But I'll make it to the top before I fall again
This one step is the solution to hundreds of my problems
Screw what all of you think
I will let my faith define me.

Only In Name

Beauty in one's eye
Is beauty to withhold
Not as if it were intentional
Not one person sees the same
Beauty is beauty
But only in name.

I'm My Own Demon

Can't think
Can't sleep
It's a dream
But it's real to me
I shout and scream
Leave me, beast
But little did I know
The beast is me.

Writing

Flow through me
Soul, heart and mind combined
Tell of passions
Or a sweet kiss
A tale of all the pain
Tell it all
Flow through me and out my pen
Speak and say what you're too afraid aloud
Words that don't easily come to me
Flow when I get to writing.

Love Beyond Time A Comedy of Divine Connection

Kayumba David and Rachael Nyarangi

Published by Kayumba David, 2024.

LOVE BEYOND TIME A COMEDY OF DIVINE CONNECTION

First edition. October 25, 2024.

Written by Kayumba David and Rachael Nyarangi.

Also by Kayumba David

1

Grow a Backbone and Walk out of an Abusive Marriage

Standalone

Grow a Backbone and Walk out of an Abusive Marriage

HARVESTING ILLUSIONS:The Global Greed and the Pan-African Paradox

Hope and Healing: A Chaplain's Handbook

HOW TO FAIL A CONTINENT: THE WESTERN GUIDE TO SUPPORTING DICTATORS AND LOOTING RESOURCES IN AFRICA

REVERSING TYPE 2 DIABETES NATURALLY

Visas: The Irony of Freedom

A MEETING WITH MAJESTY: THE KING'S CALL TO HUMANITY

A MEETING WITH MAJESTY: THE KING'S CALL TO HUMANITY

Visas: The Irony of Freedom

Grow a Backbone and Walk Out: The Guide to Escaping Your Abusive Marriage
Love Beyond Time A Comedy of Divine Connection
Silent Complicity: State Sovereignty, Global Inaction, and the Rwandan Genocide
Bridging the Rift: A Pacifist Vision for the Israel-Palestine Future

Watch for more at www.zcews.org.

Also by Rachael Nyarangi

1

Grow a Backbone and Walk out of an Abusive Marriage

Standalone

Grow a Backbone and Walk out of an Abusive Marriage
Grow a Backbone and Walk Out: The Guide to Escaping Your
Abusive Marriage
Love Beyond Time A Comedy of Divine Connection

Table of Contents

Love Beyond Time A Comedy of Divine Connection 1

Introduction 4

Chapter Nine | Following Your Dream 33

Chapter Ten | Choice Beyond Peer Pressure 35

Chapter Thirteen | The Judgment of Society (Or, How to Survive Unsolicited Opinions) 45

Chapter Fourteen | Constitutional Rights and the Gospel According to Common Sense 48

About the Authors 64

This is a love story with humor, sarcasm, and two
people who couldn't care less about society's rules. And
as you'll see, it's the kind of love that doesn't end,
because how could it?

Dedication

To everyone who's ever had that one friend—the one whose mere presence turns life into a sitcom, filled with laughter, a bit of drama, and a lot of *Wait, what just happened?* This one's for you, and for all the unbreakable bonds that leave the world utterly confused.

Preface

Love is a mystery. Sometimes it's bound by romance, other times, it's wrapped in friendship, and every now and then, it becomes something beyond both—a connection so deep, even the universe leans in to understand. And the best part? This isn't your usual love story.

What we have here is a bond that defies all labels, confounds onlookers, and endures through thick and thin—surviving scandal, a self-important narcissist, and enough rumors to power a dozen tabloids. This is a love story with humor, sarcasm, and two people who couldn't care less about society's rules. And as you'll see, it's the kind of love that doesn't end, because how could it?

So, here's a tip: Buckle up, and get ready for a hilarious ride through the story of two people who dared to forge a connection the world couldn't define.

Introduction

Welcome to a love story unlike any other, set against the vibrant backdrop of Nairobi in 1999. Here, amidst the bustling streets filled with honking matatus and the tantalizing aroma of street food, two souls find each other in a whirlwind of laughter, music, and chaos. This is a tale of resilience, an exploration of love's mysterious depths, and a celebration of the quirky bonds that defy definition.

Our protagonists, The Songbird and The Quiet One, navigate the complexities of friendship and romance while facing off against a villain of their own making: The Narcissist. This story captures the essence of true love, filled with humor and unexpected twists that will keep you laughing, pondering, and perhaps even shedding a tear or two.

As you journey through these pages, you'll discover that love is not merely a feeling but an adventure—one that thrives in laughter, challenges, and the courage to stand tall against adversity. Join us as we explore the depths of a bond so rare that even unicorns would be envious, proving that true love is indeed timeless, boundless, and fiercely resilient.

So sit back, relax, and prepare to be entertained by a saga that celebrates the magic of human connection. And remember: in the face of drama and chaos, laughter really is the best medicine.

Chapter One

The Beginning (Or, How to Find Your Soulmate in a City of Matatus)

It was Nairobi in 1999, a city that doesn't so much sleep as it occasionally blinks, checks its phone, and then goes right back to bustling. The city wasn't just alive—it was *vibrant*. Matatus barreled through the streets with the kind of confidence only vehicles that defy road safety regulations can muster. They came in every color, plastered with graffiti of everything from Michael Jordan dunking to Biblical verses written with *creative* spelling. These metal beasts carried passengers who often rode as if it were the last ride they'd ever take, clutching their bags, elbows, and maybe their last prayers.

The streets were peppered with vendors who hawked everything you didn't know you needed: miracle cures for ailments you didn't have, roasted maize with a crunch you could hear across the block, secondhand clothes, and piles of fruit so bright they looked like someone had cranked the saturation up a notch. Amid all this color, noise, and organized chaos, two people were about to cross paths in a way that made Nairobi itself pause for a second, take a sip of tea, and think, *Hmm, something special is about to happen.*

Meet The Songbird

The first was *The Songbird*, a gospel singer with a voice so powerful it could probably turn off a car alarm. Seriously, if you'd heard her sing, you'd understand. It wasn't just singing—it was *divine intervention*. The sort of voice that could make even the most hardened Nairobi pedestrian stop mid-stride, eyes widening, wondering if they'd accidentally stumbled into a celestial concert. If she performed in a rainstorm, you'd half-expect the clouds to clear, the sun to shine, and flowers to start blooming like they were paid to.

Her voice didn't only belong in churches. She sang anywhere and everywhere, blending in with the chaotic Nairobi soundtrack as if she'd been born from it. Even the matatus seemed to tune in, honking rhythmically to her impromptu sidewalk performances. Her audience was the city itself—the busy, the tired, the lost, and the hopeful—and she seemed to carry an invisible spotlight with her, lighting up spaces where darkness had settled for far too long.

Yet The Songbird wasn't just about her voice. She was joy and light personified. Her laugh, as frequent as the Kenyan rain, rippled through crowds, inviting smiles even from the grumpiest passerby. She had the kind of energy that made her feel like an old friend you'd just met, and her mere presence could make a stranger's day just a bit better.

And Then There Was The Quiet One

On the other side of the city was *The Quiet One*. Now, if The Songbird was all sunshine and symphonies, The Quiet One was more of a gentle breeze, the kind that nudges a leaf off a tree without anyone noticing. He had a knack for saying nothing and somehow saying everything at the same time. He was calm, as calm as someone standing on the side of a busy road and somehow not flinching every time a matatu honked within inches of them. He didn't draw attention, didn't strive to impress—he simply *was*.

He had the sort of demeanor that put you at ease instantly. No flashy clothes, no unnecessary gestures, no loud opinions. He was the type of guy you'd go to with a problem and leave with...well, still no solution, but somehow peace of mind anyway. If silence were a superpower, The Quiet One had mastered it. To him, words were like fine wine—used sparingly, with care, and only when necessary.

And it was this quiet strength, this unspoken power, that made him the perfect counterpart to The Songbird. They were as different as night and day, yet as inseparable as the city and its matatus. Where she was vibrant and luminous, he was steady and grounded. She was the sparkle, and he was the rock. Together, they struck a balance that defied logic.

The Moment of Collision

Their first meeting happened in the most Nairobi way possible: by chance. She was singing a little too loudly on a crowded street corner, her voice filling the air with a song so uplifting that people actually stopped for a moment before going about their day. He was just passing by, but something in him paused—an odd reaction for someone who usually moved through life as if he were invisible.

Without realizing it, he found himself standing among her impromptu audience, just another face in the crowd, but captivated. The Songbird's voice was like a magnet, and somehow, he was the only one affected. She turned, catching his gaze, and for a split second, the city faded away. Honking, laughter, chatter—all of it melted into a gentle hum, leaving just the two of them in a cocoon of music and quiet awe.

Now, you might expect one of them to say something profound. Perhaps The Songbird would launch into a speech about destiny, or maybe The Quiet One would let out a poetic line about the beauty of the moment. But, of course, that would be too simple. Instead, she stopped singing, raised an eyebrow, and said, "Enjoying the free concert?"

To which The Quiet One, in typical fashion, gave a small smile and replied, "Only because it's free."

And that was it. Just a few words exchanged, but something profound had already happened. They had connected in a way that felt like the punchline of a joke only they understood, a joke that would keep going, getting funnier as time passed.

A Connection Beyond Words

From that moment on, they shared a bond that went beyond labels or simple explanations. It was as if they had their own private language—one that needed no words and didn't conform to any societal norms. Friends? Maybe. Something more? Definitely. But words weren't necessary for them; they had their own rhythm, their own silent understanding that even they couldn't put into words.

Together, they roamed the streets of Nairobi, the Songbird singing her heart out and The Quiet One nodding along, sometimes contributing with a chuckle or a look that said more than a novel ever could. They would people-watch, making up absurd backstories for the strangers they saw, laughing as if they'd just witnessed the world's greatest comedy sketch.

Where she found beauty, he found balance. Where she noticed the dramatic, he saw the calm. They spent hours like this, talking about everything and nothing, laughing at jokes that would make no sense to anyone else, and finding joy in the little things—like the way the matatu drivers swore they'd shave a minute off their commute times by swerving through traffic like it was a personal racetrack.

A City That Watched in Amusement

People noticed them, of course. How could they not? Nairobi is a city that never misses a thing. The gossip-mongers and market vendors started calling them "The Odd Pair." The songbird and the silent guy. The bright spark and the steady flame. They didn't know what to make of them, but they sensed there was something *more* there. Some people were convinced they were in love; others thought they were siblings or perhaps co-conspirators in some wildly unlikely scheme.

But for The Songbird and The Quiet One, definitions didn't matter. They didn't need labels, explanations, or even confirmation. Their bond was something rare and unexplainable, something even they didn't fully understand. And honestly? They didn't need to. It was enough to just *be*.

In a city of miracles, mangoes, and matatus, The Songbird and The Quiet One had found something truly special—a connection beyond words, beyond labels, beyond the usual conventions. They didn't know what the future held, and they didn't need to. For now, it was just enough to share their silent jokes, their soft laughter, and their gentle presence, side by side.

And so, in the midst of Nairobi's endless bustle, a love story that wasn't really a love story began. One that didn't need grand declarations or over-the-top gestures. Just a quiet nod, a knowing smile, and the warmth of two souls who had, by some miracle or accident, found each other.

Chapter Two

Enter The Narcissist (Cue Villain Music)

It's true that every hero's journey needs a villain—someone so obsessed with their own brilliance that they actually think they're capable of taking on the very universe itself. And in this story, that villain was The Narcissist. He strutted onto the scene with the confidence of a peacock and the subtlety of a stampeding rhino, convinced he was about to steal the show. But there's a twist: his only actual talent was making grand plans with an execution strategy that was...questionable, to say the least.

From the moment he entered The Songbird's life, he envisioned himself as her *savior* and *manager*, like some kind of music industry mogul without any of the credentials. He had the smirk of a man who believed his own hype and the pep of a guy who had read every motivational quote on the internet but completely ignored the practical advice. Soon enough, he began dropping not-so-subtle hints that he could *guide* her gospel career, *enhance* her online presence, and *manage* her resources for a small "administrative fee."

The Plot to Control The Songbird's Voice

The Narcissist wasn't content with simply standing in the background; he needed to be front and center, as if he were the reason her voice was enchanting audiences. He'd heard of this new thing called *YouTube* and immediately saw an opportunity—not for The Songbird, but for himself. He envisioned an empire of content, with her as the talent and himself as the mastermind. His pitch was simple: with *his* guidance, *her* voice would reach millions. She'd be a star, and he'd be the genius behind it all.

There was just one hitch: The Songbird didn't need him to reach her fans. She already had a dedicated following, both in person and online, people who came to her not because of flashy production, but because of the authenticity of her voice. And no one—not even a self-proclaimed genius with dollar signs in his eyes—could fake that. The Narcissist tried to convince her that *he* was the key to her success, that without his grand ideas, her voice would never reach its "full potential."

However, every time he attempted to assert control, he found himself thwarted by a reality he couldn't escape: the internet didn't care about him. YouTube wasn't a puppet on his strings; in fact, it was perfectly happy giving The Songbird a platform without his input at all.

Sabotage: The Master Plan That Wasn't

Undeterred, The Narcissist went from attempting to control her career to outright sabotage. In his mind, if he couldn't *own* her success, he'd prevent her from having any. He even tried to guilt her into removing some of her videos, claiming that without *his* "branding strategy," her work lacked the "polish" she supposedly needed.

But The Songbird saw through it. She understood that her music wasn't about aesthetics or branding; it was about honesty, something The Narcissist couldn't grasp if it hit him over the head. And The Quiet One? Well, he just chuckled quietly as The Narcissist worked himself into a frenzy trying to control what he couldn't.

In a final, desperate attempt, The Narcissist hinted that he knew people who could "help her find success" if only she'd let him guide her and cut ties with those who didn't "support her vision." Translation? Get rid of The Quiet One. But, of course,

The Songbird wasn't fooled. She knew that The Quiet One's quiet wisdom was worth more than The Narcissist's loud promises ever would be.

The Songbird's Victory

In the end, The Songbird's career didn't need him. Her talent didn't need him. Even her YouTube videos didn't need his "professional touch." The people saw through his smoke and mirrors and tuned in for what they actually wanted: her music, her voice, her spirit.

After weeks of trying to muscle his way into the spotlight, The Narcissist was forced to accept the bitter truth: The Songbird's voice belonged to her, and no amount of smooth talk, sabotage, or manipulation would ever change that. Her audience wasn't there for his "vision." They were there for her voice—the one thing he had no control over.

As his grand plans fizzled out, The Narcissist finally faded into the background, all bluster and no results. The Quiet One, standing by her side with a smirk that said *told you so*, watched as she soared higher than ever, free from the constraints of someone who thought he was the center of the universe. And The Songbird? She sang louder, clearer, and stronger than ever. Because in the end, her voice was untouchable—her gift to the world, unbound and unbroken.

Chapter Three
A Bond So Rare, Even Unicorns Are Jealous

The Quiet One and The Songbird had a bond that was, well, confusing. People tried to understand it—some even made little flowcharts and hypotheses. Were they friends? Were they in love? Were they two undercover agents on some secret mission to take over Nairobi's music scene? Nobody knew for sure, and if you asked them, they'd just laugh and carry on as if being each other's "person" was as natural as breathing.

Their connection was so pure, so unapologetically real, that people just couldn't handle it. They didn't hold hands and make grand displays of affection, and they didn't plaster each other's faces all over social media. Instead, they had a shared language—a single raised eyebrow, a knowing smirk, a snort of laughter that could carry entire conversations without a single word. *Telepathy? Probably,* people whispered, half-seriously.

The Confusing Nature of a Good Thing

The Quiet One and The Songbird's bond puzzled people to no end. They'd have entire conversations with nothing but eye contact, which led to all sorts of wild assumptions. Some thought they were old souls, reincarnated from a past life where they'd probably met in ancient Egypt as Pharaoh and High Priestess.

Others decided they were modern-day prophets, obviously communicating through some divine frequency only they could hear. And, of course, the neighborhood aunties were convinced they were secretly married. If someone happened to ask, "So, what exactly *are* you two?" The Quiet One would simply smile in a way that suggested he knew the answer but had no intention of sharing it, and The Songbird would laugh, usually adding, "We're... a limited edition."

One day, a bold bystander finally asked, "Why don't you two ever define what you are?" The Quiet One thought for a second and then replied, "It's like trying to put a label on air." To which The Songbird added, "Besides, labels are for luggage, not people."

The answer left their curious friend more puzzled than ever, and that's exactly the way they liked it.

Enter The Narcissist's Dilemma

Now, if there was one person who couldn't stand the mystery, it was The Narcissist. He watched their effortless connection like a chef watching someone butcher a recipe. To him, this "bond" they had was a fortress—a high-walled, stone-laden, fortified fortress of loyalty that he had no way to infiltrate. Every time he attempted to insert himself between them, he found himself shut out, like an uninvited guest at a VIP party.

He'd throw around accusations as if casting a spell: *"They must be in some secret pact,"* he'd mutter. *"She's under his influence!"* he'd say, waving his hands dramatically. To The Narcissist, there had to be a reason—*any* reason—why The Songbird trusted The Quiet One over him. He saw their bond as an obstacle to his grand plans, a fortress he needed to conquer if he was ever to be the "chosen one" in The Songbird's world.

Naturally, he tried every trick in the book to break this "spell" of loyalty. He'd drop not-so-subtle hints that The Quiet One was "holding her back," that she needed people who could elevate her career, people with "connections." He'd say things like, "You need someone who really understands the industry, someone who knows how to navigate the world of fame." And, as if on cue, The Quiet One would roll his eyes so hard they nearly got stuck.

An Attempted Coup (or So He Thought)

The Narcissist was nothing if not persistent. At one point, he decided to throw an entire "intervention" party for The Songbird, complete with a long speech, balloons, and even a banner that read, "Choose Wisely." No one was sure what the banner meant, but The Narcissist stood in front of it with the gravitas of a military general about to announce a battle strategy. He solemnly informed her that, for the sake of her career, she needed to "evaluate her relationships." "In fact," he said, pausing for maximum effect, "there are some people in your life who are just dead weight."

To everyone's surprise (well, maybe not everyone's), The Songbird looked him dead in the eye, raised an eyebrow, and replied, "You're right. I was just thinking I need to cut back on unnecessary noise."

The Quiet One didn't even bother to hide his laughter. Meanwhile, The Narcissist stood there, momentarily speechless, which was a truly rare event. He huffed and puffed, realizing that, once again, his schemes had backfired. It was clear that this fortress of loyalty he so despised wasn't something he could break, and he hated it. For the first time in his life, he was *irrelevant*, and the only person who didn't seem to care was, well... everyone else.

The Unicorns' Envy

The bond between The Quiet One and The Songbird was one even the mythical creatures of the world envied. Unicorns, rumored to be the gold standard for rare beauty, had nothing on them. Their bond was a rare treasure, preserved in the mundane moments, a connection that made no sense but was impossible to ignore. People who met them found themselves drawn into the magic, an unbreakable friendship that defied every category.

Their mutual understanding was so strong that if The Songbird walked into a room with a worried look, The Quiet One would know exactly what it meant and where to find the solution. They could communicate in shrugs, eye rolls, and half-smiles, leaving onlookers baffled and even more intrigued. It was the kind of connection that had people convinced there must be something deeper, something truly special—because there was.

It was simple, really. They didn't need titles or labels because they weren't limited by them. They were each other's person, and it didn't matter what anyone else thought. Theirs was a connection that needed no name, no explanation—just space to breathe.

The Narcissist's Ultimate Defeat

And so, despite his best efforts, The Narcissist could do nothing to wedge himself between The Quiet One and The Songbird. He couldn't break their friendship, couldn't insert himself into their rare and beautifully undefined connection, and certainly couldn't charm his way into the fortress of trust they'd built around each other. The Narcissist huffed and puffed, tried every trick he knew, but in the end, he realized the one thing he could never control: a bond as rare as theirs was beyond his reach.

For the world, it remained a mystery. And that's just the way The Quiet One and The Songbird liked it.

Chapter Four

A Bond So Rare, Even Unicorns Are Jealous

The Quiet One and The Songbird had a connection that was as real as it was unconventional—and the fact that The Quiet One was, well, significantly older only made their friendship all the more intriguing. He had a calm, steady presence that could only come from decades of life experience, a quiet wisdom that radiated with the subtlety of a sunbeam through old stained glass. The Songbird, on the other hand, was young, vibrant, and with a voice that seemed to channel the heavens. To most, their connection was strange but beautiful, an alignment of spirits that needed no explanation.

But, of course, The Narcissist wasn't "most people." To him, the relationship between The Songbird and The Quiet One made about as much sense as a flying elephant. He couldn't wrap his mind around it—he'd even stayed up one night trying to map out how a young, budding gospel singer and an octogenarian with an endless supply of patience had ended up in what he assumed had to be a "mysterious love affair." For someone with an imagination like The Narcissist, this bond was ripe for gossip and absurd assumptions. Surely, there had to be a scandal somewhere in there! He was certain there was a hidden romance, a secret rendezvous that he could reveal with just the right amount of prodding.

An Obsession with the Age Gap

The Narcissist simply couldn't let it go. Every time he saw The Quiet One sitting peacefully next to The Songbird at her performances, he'd mutter to himself, "What is it about this old man?!" Surely, The Quiet One had to have some kind of "angle" in this. After all, in The Narcissist's world, nothing came without strings attached, least of all relationships.

One day, in his most brazen attempt at subtlety, he asked, "So, *is he, like...* family?" giving her an exaggerated wink. The Songbird just laughed, shook her head, and replied, "In the ways that matter, yes. But he's also my friend, my ally, my... compass, if you will." The Narcissist's eyebrow twitched in confusion. *Compass?* Was she speaking in metaphors now? He threw up his hands and gave a loud sigh, convinced she was just avoiding the "truth."

Failed Investigations and Unsolved Mysteries

In his relentless pursuit of "the truth," The Narcissist took to spreading rumors, slyly nudging others to question their bond as well. *"Isn't it odd, though?"* he'd say, shaking his head as if he was doing them all a favor by "raising awareness" of this unconventional friendship. He'd look around the room, wide-eyed, as if waiting for the inevitable agreement from those he saw as his future "allies" in breaking the truth wide open. His theories ranged from the outrageous (*secret lovers?*) to the downright absurd (*undercover spies?*). No angle was too strange for him to consider, no rumor too silly for him to fuel.

The Narcissist had even once approached The Quiet One in the middle of a conversation with The Songbird, interrupting with, "So, aren't you, you know, a little old for all this?" The Quiet One blinked, barely glancing up from his tea, before replying in his usual calm manner, "Old for friendship? Well, I hope not. But if so, I'd like a refund on all these years, please." The Songbird had to stifle her laughter, while The Narcissist retreated with a frustrated huff, grumbling about "cryptic answers" and "old man wisdom."

When Gossip Backfires

Determined as ever to "expose" whatever mysterious "affair" he thought was happening, The Narcissist took his campaign to a new level, dropping hints about this so-called "relationship" every chance he got. The Songbird, however, was unbothered. She simply laughed off the rumors, dismissing them with a light-hearted wave. As far as she was concerned, people could think what they wanted. But The Narcissist soon realized his tactics were backfiring, especially when people began to say, "You know, it's rare to find a friendship like that. Almost makes you wish you had one too, doesn't it?"

Despite all his efforts, The Narcissist had failed. He couldn't conquer what he didn't understand, and he couldn't break what was unbreakable. He fumed, pacing in circles and muttering to himself like a thwarted cartoon villain, defeated by a bond so rare and unique that even he had to admit—begrudgingly—it was something special.

A Friendship That Outshone All Doubt

The Quiet One and The Songbird carried on with their friendship, delighting in the peace that came from a connection unburdened by definition. They were each other's person, and that's all they needed to be. The people who tried to make sense of it eventually gave up, except for The Narcissist, who never quite recovered from the mystery of it all. He could label and scheme all he wanted, but their bond remained a beautiful enigma, a rare and timeless connection that required no explanation, just like the best things in life.

Chapter Five

The Narcissist's Master Plan (Or, How to Fail at Everything)

The Narcissist, ever the schemer, had one final trick up his sleeve. Realizing his previous attempts to undermine The Songbird and The Quiet One had fizzled out like a damp firecracker, he decided to amplify the drama with a fresh dose of his favorite tactic: projection. He'd point the finger at them so fiercely, he thought, that no one would ever look too closely at him.

The Narcissist, after all, had his own "activities" that he desperately wanted to keep out of the spotlight—indiscretions, failed promises, and moral lapses that were as numerous as they were egregious. And so, in what he considered a stroke of pure brilliance, he aimed to deflect any future blame for his own questionable behavior by orchestrating a dramatic narrative around The Songbird and The Quiet One.

A "Scandal" to Outshine His Own Sins

The Narcissist crafted an elaborate tale, accusing The Songbird and The Quiet One of a sordid, scandalous connection that, as he told it, would "shock" everyone. He spun his web of lies with incredible detail, throwing in phrases like "betrayal" and "secret pacts," hoping to spark enough intrigue and suspicion that people would forget to look into his own increasingly shady reputation.

The more elaborate his accusations, the more he hoped to bury his own misdeeds under layers of fabricated drama. He'd sweep into conversations with wild eyes, whispering loudly about the supposed "truth" he'd uncovered. *"Did you hear? There's more going on with them than you'd ever imagine,"* he'd declare with an ominous nod, as if he were some kind of amateur detective.

The truth, of course, was that his "drama" was nothing but a smokescreen—a carefully crafted distraction meant to hide his own, let's say, "after-hours activities." From failed financial deals to promises that had backfired, The Narcissist's history was dotted with instances he'd rather keep buried. And so, the more he could twist the focus onto The Songbird and The Quiet One, the safer he felt.

Drama So Contrived, Even Soap Operas Would Reject It

His accusations grew wilder by the day. He even began assigning roles to the people around him, as if they were all players in a great soap opera he was scripting himself. He'd stage "confrontations" with dramatic pauses, exaggerating his shock and sorrow, trying to appear the heartbroken witness to the "betrayal" of their bond. But while he thought he was crafting Shakespearean-level drama, it came off more like a low-budget TV special.

"I saw them once," he'd declare to anyone within earshot, "in a secret meeting by the fountain, whispering to each other. I'm telling you, there's something dark at work here." He'd shake his head as if he were gravely concerned. Most people listened with one eyebrow raised, struggling to contain their laughter at his ridiculous antics.

The Quiet One and The Songbird: Unmoved and Amused

While The Narcissist ran himself ragged with his fabricated drama, The Songbird and The Quiet One remained hilariously oblivious. Every time a rumor reached their ears, they'd shrug, exchange a smirk, and carry on. They could see what The Narcissist was doing, but their bond was so solid that these melodramatic attempts were little more than background noise.

"You know," The Quiet One once mused, "if he put this much energy into something constructive, he could probably achieve something."

The Songbird laughed. "Too late for that," she replied. "Let him burn himself out. He's the only one who believes his own stories at this point."

Indeed, The Narcissist's exaggerated tales soon became the punchline of every joke. The more he tried to weave his tangled web, the less anyone took him seriously. His "drama" had lost its shock value, and people started noticing inconsistencies in his stories. Meanwhile, his own less-than-honorable escapades were quietly coming to light, no matter how hard he tried to keep them in the dark.

When the Curtain Falls

In the end, The Narcissist's scheme unraveled just like his reputation. As the public grew weary of his constant, implausible tales, they began to question his motives. And just as he feared, people began looking more closely into his own behavior. The irony was sweet: his attempts to ruin others' reputations only served to expose his own.

One by one, his dirty secrets trickled out—small at first, but gradually forming a tide of revelations that no amount of finger-pointing could stop. All those misdeeds he'd hoped to gloss over with his "master plan" were now the talk of the town, leaving him no choice but to retreat from the limelight he'd once so eagerly sought.

As for The Songbird and The Quiet One? They laughed, carrying on with their friendship as if nothing had happened. And in the end, that was the ultimate victory: while The Narcissist faded away in disgrace, they remained standing, unbothered, their bond still strong and untouched by the storm he'd tried—and failed—to create.

Chapter Six

Laughter—The Best Defense Against Drama and Narcissists

When life throws a narcissist and a mountain of drama your way, there's really only one way to survive it: laughter. And The Songbird and The Quiet One had practically turned laughter into an art form. From the very first whisper of a rumor to the most outrageous accusations, their secret weapon had always been humor. Why cry when you could laugh so hard that tears streamed down your face and your sides hurt?

To The Songbird and The Quiet One, each rumor was like a gift—a ridiculous, wildly over-exaggerated story, carefully wrapped by The Narcissist for their entertainment. Some people might have found the whole ordeal exhausting, but they saw it as endless comedic material. The more elaborate and convoluted The Narcissist's schemes grew, the funnier they found them.

Drama, a Side of Hysteria, and One Big Belly Laugh

If The Narcissist had known how many giggle fits he'd inspired, he probably would've dropped his "mastermind" act and gotten a new hobby. But to The Songbird and The Quiet One, he was their personal (unpaid) comic, constantly churning out new material for their amusement. Each accusation became a punchline, and each exaggerated rumor another chapter in their running joke. They would imitate The Narcissist's dramatic hand gestures and his "gravely serious" expressions in perfect, exaggerated detail, sending each other into fits of laughter in the process.

"Did you hear?" The Songbird would say, barely holding back a laugh. "Apparently, we're secretly meeting at 2 a.m. by the fountain to discuss the weather."

The Quiet One would nod solemnly, "Yes, and word on the street is we're forming a secret society—just the two of us—to overthrow... uh, reality?"

"Obviously," The Songbird would reply, breaking into laughter. "It's the only logical conclusion, really."

The Poisoned Minds of Relatives

But as The Songbird and The Quiet One turned their misfortunes into a comedy routine, The Narcissist was busy implementing his master plan. Realizing that direct attacks weren't working, he decided to take a more insidious route. He began poisoning the minds of The Songbird's relatives, spinning tales so outrageous that they could've qualified for an award in the "Most Ridiculous Accusation" category.

"You know, your niece is quite the character," he would start innocently enough at family gatherings. *"I think she's taken quite a liking to The Quiet One. Some say she's plotting something sinister!"* He would lean in conspiratorially, eyes wide, as if divulging state secrets.

And just like that, the drama escalated from light-hearted absurdity to a full-blown family fiasco. The relatives—bless their hearts—were immediately hooked. They didn't see the humor in The Narcissist's stories; they saw a threat. Suddenly, The Songbird wasn't just a talented gospel singer; she was a "dangerous individual," and in The Narcissist's world, dangerous people had to be stopped.

Conspiracies and Family Meetings

Family gatherings, once filled with laughter and joy, turned into covert meetings filled with whispered conspiracies about The Songbird's alleged plots against The Narcissist. *"Have you seen the way she looks at him?"* one aunt would say, casting a suspicious glance. *"It's like she's plotting an assassination!"*

"Assassination?" another relative would chime in, eyebrows raised. "But she's a gospel singer! Shouldn't she be plotting to save souls instead?"

Well, no one had ever accused The Narcissist of being particularly logical.

The cousins began to pick sides, creating a drama of their own as they engaged in heated debates over dinner tables about The Songbird's intentions. Would she really try to take down The Narcissist? Was her soothing voice merely a cover for a sinister agenda? How could someone so talented be up to no good?

But while The Songbird's family swirled in confusion and drama, The Songbird herself remained blissfully unaware of her newfound reputation. Meanwhile, The Quiet One took to eavesdropping with the utmost dedication, thoroughly entertained by the absurdity. It was like reality TV, but live and with no commercial breaks.

Turning the Tables with Humor

Of course, The Quiet One and The Songbird soon caught wind of what was happening, thanks to a casual, accidentally overheard conversation. One evening, while they were enjoying a particularly hearty laugh over takeout, a particularly animated relative of The Songbird burst through the door, eyes wide with concern.

"Rachael!" she exclaimed, *"What are you planning? We need to talk about your intentions with that man!"*

The Songbird blinked in confusion, then burst into laughter. *"My intentions? I'm planning to buy him dinner this Friday! Would you like to join us?"*

The relative looked flustered, unsure if it was a jest or a genuine invitation.

"Dinner? With him?" she stammered. "But what if he's plotting against you?!"

"Oh, dear aunt, if he were plotting anything, it would probably involve stealing my last piece of cake!" The Songbird replied, grinning.

And just like that, the conversation shifted from intense seriousness to peals of laughter. The relatives could only shake their heads in disbelief. How could someone so talented be such a threat, especially if she was joking about cake?

The Laughter Effect

As the weeks passed, The Songbird and The Quiet One found that laughter was the best antidote for the toxicity surrounding them. They even turned the whole family drama into a skit they performed during family gatherings, complete with ridiculous costumes and exaggerated impersonations of The Narcissist.

"And here we have the misunderstood artist!" The Songbird would exclaim, twirling in a way that would've made any ballerina proud, mimicking The Narcissist's dramatic flair. *"Who believes I'm secretly plotting his demise!"*

The relatives finally began to see the humor in the situation, slowly untangling themselves from The Narcissist's web of lies. They started questioning their own fears and perceptions. If anything, they realized The Songbird had a heart full of love, laughter, and music—not plots and conspiracies.

In the end, while The Narcissist continued to swirl in a tornado of his own making, The Songbird and The Quiet One emerged stronger, their laughter resonating like the sweetest melody against the backdrop of chaos. After all, in the grand tapestry of life, laughter is a thread that stitches bonds tighter, creating a fabric of resilience, joy, and an impenetrable friendship.

Chapter Seven

The Narcissist Fades Away (Spoiler: No One Misses Him)

As with all things hollow, The Narcissist's hold on The Songbird's life began to fade. It wasn't dramatic; there were no epic monologues or grand exit speeches, just the slow, painful realization that his charm had all the staying power of a helium balloon—impressive for a moment, but destined to float away, leaving nothing but deflated sadness behind.

When his schemes failed to produce the reaction he craved—specifically, any reaction at all—he moved on to his next stage, or at least the one he imagined he deserved. This was a man who believed himself to be the sun in the solar system of relationships, but as it turns out, he was more like that weird little asteroid that nobody noticed until it was time to clean up the backyard.

The Great Disappearing Act

The day he left was eerily quiet. It was like a scene from a poorly written soap opera where the villain simply walks off into the sunset without so much as a "goodbye." One minute he was there, and the next, poof! Gone! No fireworks, no dramatic music, just the sound of crickets and the collective sigh of relief from everyone who had ever been within earshot of his grandiose tales.

The Songbird and The Quiet One, meanwhile, didn't even notice his absence at first. They were too busy enjoying their lives. Their days returned to their usual rhythm, punctuated by laughter and impromptu karaoke sessions that could probably wake the neighbors—and if they did, well, they were well aware that The Songbird's voice could make even the grumpiest neighbor crack a smile (or at least a grimace, which was a win in their book).

Life After The Narcissist

With The Narcissist's shadow gone, it felt as if someone had finally pulled the curtain back on a stage that had been draped in tacky, outdated decor. Suddenly, the world was brighter, the air fresher, and The Songbird could finally belt out her tunes without worrying about "the audience" being scandalized by her "mysterious friendship" with The Quiet One.

"Hey, did you ever think we could have a duet called 'Bye Bye, Bloaty'?" The Songbird teased one afternoon, flinging her arms wide as if addressing an imaginary crowd.

"Oh, absolutely! We could open with a heartfelt ballad about how to avoid bad company!" The Quiet One replied with a grin, his eyes twinkling with mischief.

As they continued to riff off each other, their bond remained as solid as ever, having weathered storms, rumors, and drama with humor, resilience, and an unspoken understanding. They even made a sport out of recalling The Narcissist's outlandish tales, giggling over the absurdity of it all.

"Remember when he tried to convince everyone that you were plotting my assassination?" The Songbird asked, trying to stifle a laugh.

"Oh yes! And he claimed I was a secret agent!" The Quiet One replied, rolling his eyes dramatically. *"I mean, if I were a secret agent, would I really be hanging out at matatus in Nairobi?"*

"Exactly! I would've expected you to be in a tuxedo, sipping martinis!" The Songbird added, laughing heartily. *"Not slumming it with a gospel singer!"*

The Celebration of Freedom

To celebrate their newfound freedom from The Narcissist's theatrics, they decided to throw a little party—just the two of them, with a playlist featuring everything from classic gospel hymns to guilty pleasure pop songs. It was a celebration of joy, laughter, and the fact that they no longer had to dodge the slings and arrows of outrageous accusations.

As they danced and sang like no one was watching (which, honestly, was true because their neighbors had long learned to avoid their shenanigans), they reveled in the sweetness of peace. Their friendship, built on laughter and mutual respect, flourished even more.

"Who needs a narcissist when we have the finest karaoke setup in Nairobi?" The Quiet One declared, holding up an imaginary microphone. "Let's make a pact: no more toxic people in our lives! Only good vibes and well-timed punchlines!"

"Deal! Let's write a song about it! Maybe call it 'Toxic Exclusion Zone'?" The Songbird suggested, her eyes sparkling with inspiration.

The Aftermath and the Reflections

Weeks turned into months, and life continued on blissfully, without The Narcissist's shadow looming over them. They even noticed that some of The Songbird's relatives began to warm up to her again, having realized the absurdity of their previous beliefs. Rumors dissipated faster than a poorly made balloon animal, and laughter filled the void that The Narcissist had tried to create.

As they looked back, The Songbird and The Quiet One often chuckled about how absurdly dramatic life could be. They realized that, sometimes, the best way to deal with difficult people was to laugh them away.

"I think we need to start an anti-narcissist club," The Quiet One mused one day, "complete with laughter therapy and a 'no drama' policy."

"Oh, absolutely! We could even have membership cards, like the 'Don't Be Like Him' club," The Songbird chimed in, laughing. "Our motto? 'Life's too short for bad company and bad music!'"

And with that, they clinked their glasses, toasting to a future filled with laughter, music, and friendship, leaving The Narcissist—who was, let's be honest, now just a faded memory—far behind.

Chapter Nine
Following Your Dream

As life unfolded, it often posed the question: **What do you truly want?** For The Songbird, the answer was as clear as a sunny Nairobi day: she wanted to share her music with the world. Her dream burned within her like a pot of ugali on a hot stove, ready to overflow with delicious potential. But chasing dreams in a city buzzing with distractions, matatu horns, and vendors shouting "Mango! Fresh mango!" was no small feat.

"You know," The Quiet One said one evening while watching The Songbird belt out a tune to an audience of indifferent pigeons and one slightly confused goat, "you could always become a matatu conductor. They seem to enjoy singing, especially the ones that start dancing to the music on their own!"

She shot him a playful glare. "Thanks, but I'd prefer not to share my vocal talents with an audience that has a propensity to throw loose change at me—or worse, ask me to rap along to some questionable lyrics."

With a grin, he nodded. "Fair enough. But really, don't let anyone dull your shine. The world needs your music, even if that world sometimes sounds like a matatu blasting bongo flava."

Armed with dreams and an unwavering belief in each other, they ventured into the heart of Nairobi. The Songbird sang in the streets, often improvising lyrics about the joys of street food and the absurdity of traffic jams. "Matatus don't have brakes! Just a prayer!" she would belt out, drawing laughter from her makeshift audience.

Despite the inevitable critics lurking like hawkers with overripe bananas, The Songbird learned to filter the noise. "For every doubter, there's a fan waiting to be discovered," she quipped, tossing her hair dramatically. The passersby started to cheer her on—not just for her voice, but for her authenticity and uncanny ability to find humor in the hustle of city life.

One day, an elderly woman approached her, shaking her head with a mixture of disbelief and admiration. "Child," she said, "you have a voice that could wake the dead! Do you have a matatu to drive yet?"

"No, Mama! But I have dreams bigger than a whole street market!" The Songbird replied, laughing.

And with each passing day, she attracted an audience that cheered her on—not just for her music, but for her ability to turn everyday challenges into hilarious ballads.

Chapter Ten
Choice Beyond Peer Pressure

Now, let's talk about the inevitable—peer pressure. It's the pesky little voice that whispers, "Do what everyone else is doing; it's easier!" In Nairobi, this often translates into trying to fit into the latest trends, like balancing an avocado on your head while taking a selfie.

One day, while sipping chai at their favorite café—where the waiter knew their usual orders better than they did—The Quiet One brought up a conversation that many young people dread. "You know, it's easy to get caught up in what others expect of you. But what about your own dreams? What do you really want?"

The Songbird raised an eyebrow, stirring her chai with dramatic flair. "Oh, you mean like that time you almost became a professional chess player because your friends thought it was cool?"

He chuckled, "Exactly! But the moment I realized I'd rather be writing stories than stuck in a chess match with a group of serious-faced individuals—who, by the way, always insisted on wearing those strange hats—I chose my own path."

She nodded, reflecting on her own choices. "Sometimes, it feels like there's an invisible script that everyone else is following, and if you stray, you're the odd one out. Like wearing sandals with socks in a city known for its fashion!"

"Or," he countered, leaning forward with mock seriousness, "you could be the leading actor in your own blockbuster. Forget the script! Write your own lines, break the fourth wall, and dance offstage whenever you like—preferably to a benga beat."

They both erupted into laughter, nearly spilling their chai. "So, you're saying I should perform spontaneous musical numbers on the streets?" she teased.

"Exactly! And when people stare, just tell them you're auditioning for a reality show called 'The Life of a Songbird.' You know how much Kenyans love a good show!"

With their shared humor as armor, they faced societal pressures head-on. They knew that staying true to oneself was the greatest rebellion of all, especially in a world that sometimes feels like a never-ending reality show of peer pressure and expectations.

Together, they danced through the noise, reminding each other that the sweetest melodies come from the heart, not from the whispers of others. As the sun set on their journey, they realized that following your dreams—while dodging peer pressure—wasn't just a choice; it was a grand adventure filled with laughter, love, and a sprinkle of African magic.

Chapter Eleven

A Love Story Without an Ending (Because Who Needs One?)

Years rolled by in a smooth, unhurried fashion, like a matatu taking its sweet time through Nairobi traffic. The bond between The Quiet One and The Songbird only grew stronger—so strong, in fact, that it could probably bench press a small car. They didn't need a fairytale ending; they just wanted the comfort of knowing that whatever they were to each other, it was real.

The Anti-Label Coalition

In a world obsessed with labels, they had formed their very own Anti-Label Coalition. "Why label ourselves?" The Quiet One would often ask, looking as serious as a cat contemplating its next nap. "I mean, we're not jam. We don't need a jar or a sticker to define what we are!"

"Exactly!" The Songbird would chirp, nodding vigorously. "Labels are for jars and overpriced clothing, not for feelings! Plus, what if we just stick with 'dynamic duo'? It has a nice ring to it, and we can definitely wear matching capes!"

With each passing year, their laughter became the glue that held them together. While the world buzzed around them, demanding categories and classifications, they embraced the beauty of ambiguity. "We're like the plot twist nobody saw coming," The Songbird declared one day, flinging her arms wide in theatrical flair. "And we're fabulous!"

The Comfort of the Everyday

Their relationship thrived in the everyday moments—the comfortable silence that stretched between them like a warm blanket, the spontaneous sing-alongs that turned mundane chores into epic concerts, and the playful banter that kept their spirits high. Who needs a grand declaration of love when you could share a knowing glance over a plate of pilau that said, "I'd share my last bite with you"?

One day, while washing dishes together, The Quiet One glanced at The Songbird and said, "You know, I could probably write an entire book on our dishwashing adventures."

The Songbird laughed, "Only if the title is *Washing Dishes: The Epic Saga of Soapy Heroics!*"

"Right? And the cover art would be us battling a mountain of dirty plates in capes and sponges."

Grand Gestures? Nah. Just Everyday Magic

Theirs wasn't a relationship that needed grand gestures. Forget bouquets of roses; they were more likely to celebrate their love with spontaneous dance-offs in the kitchen or transforming a casual stroll into an impromptu karaoke session. "What's that?" The Quiet One would say, pointing to a random passerby. "Is it a bird? Is it a plane? No, it's the *Songbird* taking the stage!"

One afternoon, while sipping on their chai at a bustling cafe, they overheard a couple at the next table. "You have to say 'I love you' at least once a day!" the woman insisted, her voice dripping with conviction.

The Quiet One and The Songbird exchanged amused glances. "Once a day?" The Quiet One whispered, "What a rookie mistake! We say it every five minutes!"

"Well, if they need help, we can offer our 'how to avoid cliché declarations' workshop!" The Songbird quipped.

An Endless Journey

Time marched on, but they never felt the need to rush into defining their connection. Theirs was a story without an ending, and frankly, who needed one? They were the couple who knew that love wasn't just about fireworks and romantic sunsets; it was about the small, unassuming moments—the quiet nights spent sharing dreams, the random adventures that turned into laughter-filled escapades, and the unwavering support that felt like a safety net woven from the threads of their friendship.

They could often be found making up silly songs about the day's adventures or composing ridiculous ballads about whatever caught their fancy. One particularly memorable tune went something like this:

"Oh, the cat who thinks he owns the couch,
And the neighbor who mows his lawn too loud,
Together we'll face the absurdity,
With love, laughter, and a cup of tea!"

Each ridiculous song was a testament to their connection—proof that they could turn even the most mundane aspects of life into cherished memories.

Forever and Always

And so they danced through life, hand in hand, hearts intertwined. Their love story was an evolving tapestry—colorful, vibrant, and beautifully intricate. It wasn't about reaching a destination; it was about enjoying the journey, savoring every twist and turn, and laughing all the way.

The Songbird and The Quiet One had created a world of their own, where the rules of love were rewritten to fit their unique narrative. They were each other's forever—without needing a label, a grand finale, or a neatly wrapped ending.

As they both often mused, "Why chase an ending when we can create our own adventures?"

And thus, their love story continued—an endless melody played in the rhythm of life, filled with laughter, companionship, and the sweet simplicity of two souls who understood each other on a level so deep, no one else could reach.

Chapter Twelve

The Suspense Continues (Because Who Doesn't Love a Little Mystery?)

And so, their story continues, just as it always has. With the clock ticking and the sun setting over Nairobi, The Songbird and The Quiet One keep laughing, sharing that rare, unspoken language that needs no translation, and living out their days with a bond that defies explanation.

But as it turns out, life in Nairobi had its own brand of intrigue—one that couldn't be contained by mere romantic escapades or karaoke duets. Oh no! There were still plenty of mysteries swirling around them, including an ongoing saga involving none other than The Narcissist himself.

The Courtroom Chronicles: A Legal Telenovela

What's a story without a little drama? After The Narcissist's failed attempts to sabotage their lives, he decided to take his melodrama to the next level. Armed with a keyboard and a misguided sense of justice, he took to social media, launching a smear campaign that would have made any soap opera villain proud.

"Can you believe this?" The Quiet One scoffed one evening as they scrolled through a timeline filled with exaggerated accusations and outright lies. "He's claiming you're plotting his demise! What's next? A tell-all book titled *Confessions of a Narcissist*?"

"Oh, please! If he had any brains, he'd realize that trying to poison my reputation is like trying to drown a fish—pointless!" The Songbird laughed, her eyes sparkling. "Besides, I'm more of a 'peace, love, and chai' kind of gal. What's he going to do? Accuse me of carrying a poison pen?"

But when The Narcissist took it to the courtroom, it became the legal equivalent of a telenovela. "Your Honor," he would declare, dramatically tossing his hands in the air, "this woman has used her voice to create a sinister symphony of hate against me!"

The court erupted in laughter. "And where's your evidence?" the judge asked, barely concealing a smirk.

"I... uh... have social media posts!" he stammered. "Proof that she and her quiet companion are up to no good!"

The Songbird and The Quiet One exchanged amused glances. "Wow," The Quiet One whispered, "he must think we're James Bond and an accomplice."

The Chicken Dance of Defeat

As the saga dragged on, it became clear that The Narcissist was not only fighting a losing battle but was also engaging in a comedy of errors. Every hearing brought a fresh round of accusations, followed by a fresh round of eye rolls from the judge. "You do realize you're only making yourself look ridiculous, right?" the judge finally said, leaning back in his chair with a bemused expression.

In the end, when the walls began to close in on him, The Narcissist had a moment of reckoning. It was as if he had finally realized that he was burning alone in a bonfire of his own making. He was the only one dancing around, chanting "victim," while everyone else was munching on popcorn, enjoying the spectacle.

"A ceasefire?" he proposed one day, his voice quaking as he approached The Songbird and The Quiet One in the courthouse hallway. "I think we should—uh—make amends."

"Make amends?" The Songbird raised an eyebrow, barely able to contain her laughter. "You mean like getting together for chai and sharing our feelings?"

"Exactly!" he squeaked, looking like a deer caught in the headlights of a matatu.

"You're serious, aren't you?" The Quiet One remarked, suppressing a grin. "You must be really tired of losing."

"Fine, I'll admit it! I'm exhausted!" The Narcissist cried, his bravado deflating faster than a popped balloon. "I didn't sign up for this court drama! I thought I'd win!"

The Great Escape

With a ceasefire officially declared (though no one quite understood what that meant), The Narcissist slinked away, leaving behind a trail of awkwardness and half-hearted apologies. He may have thought he could continue to play the victim card, but the only card he held was the joker, and the joke was on him.

As The Songbird and The Quiet One watched him disappear into the distance, they couldn't help but break into laughter. "Can you believe that guy?" The Songbird chuckled. "He really thought he could take us down!"

"Or that we'd ever need his approval," The Quiet One added, shaking his head. "He's about as relevant to our story as a cactus in a swimming pool."

Some Mysteries Are Best Left Unsolved

As the days turned into weeks and weeks into months, The Songbird and The Quiet One embraced the whispers with a chuckle. They found it amusing that their bond sparked so much intrigue, like a novel that kept readers on the edge of their seats.

And with The Narcissist out of the picture (at least for now), they were free to enjoy their lives, their laughter echoing through Nairobi, a testament to a bond that had weathered storms and outlasted the most ridiculous drama.

Some mysteries, after all, are best left unsolved. Why complicate things with explanations when laughter was the language that connected them?

One evening, as they watched the sun dip below the horizon, The Songbird turned to The Quiet One and mused, "Maybe we should start giving them something to really talk about. Like adopting a pet rock!"

"Or we could host a talent show and compete against each other. I'm pretty sure my rock stacking skills could be a hit!" he replied, his eyes twinkling with humor.

And so, as they plotted their next whimsical adventure, they knew that their story—filled with laughter, love, and a dash of mystery—was far from over.

The End?

Or maybe not. Perhaps the best part of a story like theirs is that it doesn't have to end. With every giggle, every conspiratorial glance, and every absurd plan they concocted, their bond grew stronger, weaving them deeper into the fabric of life's delightful chaos.

And in the grand tapestry of their lives, The Songbird and The Quiet One had found something extraordinary: a love story that was endless, much like their laughter.

Chapter Thirteen

The Judgment of Society (Or, How to Survive Unsolicited Opinions)

In Kenya, there are two things everyone thinks they're born qualified to do: fix a car and give advice—solicited or not. So when The Songbird's life took an unexpected turn, she was prepared for opinions to rain down on her like a December storm. The Narcissist, with all his flair for drama, knew just how to stoke the flames, spinning tales that were juicier than the morning tea at Mama Wanjiru's kibanda. Soon, everyone from neighborhood mamas to the guy at the boda boda stage was buzzing with their own take on the saga.

The rumors were so hot they practically needed their own hashtag. Auntie Mary, who knew every storyline on *Maria* by heart, practically hosted her own TV show of gossip. With a dramatic wave of her scarf, she would lean in, wide-eyed, and whisper to anyone who'd listen, "A young woman with such a strange friendship? Surely there's more to this story than meets the eye." To Auntie Mary, The Songbird's life was more thrilling than anything *Citizen TV* had to offer, and if she didn't have the truth, she filled in the blanks with all the gusto of a prime-time soap opera writer.

Then there were the religious leaders, eager to turn The Songbird's friendship into a cautionary tale. "Let us pray for this lost sheep," they'd say, nodding solemnly as if they alone could lift her out of some fabricated spiritual abyss. The whispers found their way to church committees, the women's chama, and even the market stall vendors. Strangers on matatus chimed in as well, eager to add their two cents during long traffic jams on Mombasa Road, their voices rising above the preacher selling eternal salvation for fifty shillings.

But The Songbird was no rookie in handling public drama. She knew that in Kenya, unsolicited advice is as common as "Please call me" texts. So, with a mixture of humor and resilience, she fortified herself for the storm. Her silent mantra became: "If you don't pay my bills, your opinion is just hot air." Armed with a steady reserve of eye rolls and The Quiet One's unwavering support, she faced each comment with a polite nod and a mental tally of how much tea she could sell with all these stories.

One particularly memorable encounter came from Mama Amina, the self-appointed neighborhood expert on "respectable behavior." She cornered The Songbird outside the church, wagging her finger with all the authority of a government official. "Eh, my dear, you know we only want the best for you. Why associate with questionable company? Think of your reputation!"

The Songbird smiled sweetly, managing not to laugh. "Thank you, Mama Amina, I'll keep that in mind," she said, with all the grace of a politician brushing off a scandal.

Each unsolicited opinion only made her tougher. After all, The Songbird didn't need a label, nor did she need approval. What she needed was to live freely, laugh heartily, and ignore everyone who assumed they knew her better than she knew herself. Her life was her own, not a neighborhood soap opera. So, with a quiet strength that few could understand, she carried on, laughing in the face of every whispered assumption and casting each judgmental glance aside like confetti. The drama could rage on, but The Songbird? She was simply living her life—her way.

Chapter Fourteen

Constitutional Rights and the Gospel According to Common Sense

It wasn't long before The Songbird realized there was something stronger than the village gossip, and it came with the force of legal codes and constitutional rights. While the Narcissist and his clan were busy spreading rumors like it was market day in Gikomba, she knew her dignity, choices, and peace were backed by more than just neighborhood whispers. She was bolstered by actual laws and, perhaps even more profoundly, a reliable protector: The Quiet One.

Unlike most people who saw the law as an abstract concept or a last resort, The Quiet One had unshakable faith in it. He was a silent but steadfast believer that justice, when given the proper tools, could prevail even in the trickiest of situations. And this belief was only strengthened when they encountered the mysterious yet sharp-witted lawyer, JL—a figure who seemed heaven-sent to dismantle the Narcissist's empire of lies with nothing more than truth, logic, and a hint of sarcasm.

JL, with a demeanor as steady as The Quiet One's own, was the kind of lawyer you'd want in your corner: competent, calm, and unfazed by the theatrics of small-town drama. JL came on board with the firm resolution to restore The Songbird's dignity while letting the Narcissist learn that not everyone could be swayed by his charming villainy. JL's quiet yet powerful strategy left everyone baffled; he had an uncanny way of dismantling the Narcissist's twisted narratives piece by piece until even the Narcissist himself began to lose track of his own stories.

One memorable court appearance saw JL casually lean forward, eyebrows raised, as he asked the Narcissist to clarify his claims—twice. The Narcissist, squirming in his seat and sweating as if Nairobi's January heat had suddenly risen a few notches, began stammering incoherently, unable to keep his own fabrications straight. His theatrical outbursts, so convincing in casual gossip circles, looked pitifully out of place under JL's calm scrutiny.

The Quiet One watched all of this with a barely concealed smile. To him, this was the beauty of the legal system: its power to calmly, rationally, and systematically expose lies. He had a deep trust in the process, knowing that, just like a persistent drip of water can wear down the hardest rock, the truth would eventually outshine the shadows cast by the Narcissist's endless deceit.

The Songbird couldn't help but marvel at the serendipity of it all. Not only was she armed with her own resilience and faith, but she had also been granted the unexpected blessing of JL, who saw through every smoke screen and aimed straight for the truth. With every new court session, it became clearer that the walls of the Narcissist's fabricated empire were cracking, and JL's methodical work was quickly transforming those cracks into full-on collapses.

Meanwhile, back in the neighborhood, the ever-vocal Auntie Mary and the crowd of gossipers continued to speculate on the case. "Why would anyone need a lawyer if they were truly innocent?" she whispered, barely concealing her own curiosity under a veil of righteous indignation. But JL's work spoke for itself. Slowly but surely, the judgmental crowd began to see the Narcissist's schemes for what they were—petty attempts to hold back a woman who was, in her quiet dignity, beyond his reach.

And as each day in court came to a close, The Quiet One and The Songbird would walk out, exchanging a satisfied glance. JL had taught them an invaluable lesson: that there is power in truth and resilience, and that sometimes, all it takes to dismantle an empire built on lies is a well-timed question and a lawyer who knows when to let the silence speak for itself.

Thus, with the support of The Quiet One, JL's legal prowess, and her own quiet determination, The Songbird was free to reclaim her dignity. And in that courtroom, as she watched the Narcissist's empire of deceit crumble, she felt a renewed sense of strength—a strength that came not only from the constitution, but from the divine assurance that justice, in its purest form, was always on her side.

Chapter Fifteen

The Narcissist's Empire (Or, How Not to Build a House of Cards)

While The Songbird fortified herself with truth, resilience, and a lawyer who knew his way around a courtroom, The Narcissist was busy building his empire of lies. He seemed to have turned rumor-mongering into an art form, feeding tales to any open ears with all the enthusiasm of a town crier on market day. In Kenya, where a good story is valued as much as a cup of tea, he had a willing audience. From the back pews of local churches to the noisy corners of roadside kiosks, his stories spread like gossip on a hot matatu—fast, noisy, and often overheard by people who didn't even ask.

At first, his tales captivated the neighborhood, pulling in everyone from Auntie Mary at the kiosk to Pastor Tom in the church. He was the king of his own drama series, casting himself as the misunderstood victim and The Songbird as the cunning schemer. In his stories, he was the hero of nearly biblical proportions, always just "trying to save" a troubled woman, all while valiantly suffering in silence. "Poor Narcissist," people murmured. "How much more can he take?" Auntie Mary could barely keep up with the twists; she'd practically run out of sighs and head-shakes.

But it didn't take long for the cracks in his stories to show. As any Kenyan knows, you can only stretch a lie so far before it snaps back at you like an overloaded matatu seatbelt. The unraveling began subtly. First, a neighbor raised an eyebrow, recalling an earlier version of one of his stories that didn't quite line up with his latest account. Then, a close friend, once his biggest supporter, noticed how conveniently The Narcissist shifted blame onto others in every scenario. Soon, even his most loyal followers began to see through the inconsistencies, and what had once been a gripping tale started to resemble a badly cooked stew—lumpy, unappetizing, and served cold.

To make matters worse, word on the street spread fast that JL, The Songbird's no-nonsense lawyer, was unraveling his claims one by one, like peeling the layers off a bad onion. People started whispering, "Have you heard? Even the lawyer could see through him!" The Narcissist's empire of deceit was beginning to look like a poorly constructed house of cards on a windy day. And yet, despite the visible collapse of his story, he doubled down.

Feigning indifference, The Narcissist brushed it off in public. "I don't care what they think," he'd mutter with a forced smile, though anyone could see it was starting to look more like a grimace. Every now and then, you could spot him pacing around in his compound, talking to himself as though rehearsing his latest performance. The more he denied caring, the more people noticed the faint desperation in his eyes. He was no longer the master of his carefully spun tales but a man caught in a web of his own making.

As his fabricated empire crumbled, he discovered that his once-trusted ally, pride, was now the heaviest burden he couldn't shake. Friends drifted away, the neighborhood laughter began to follow him, and the crowd of followers who had once believed his every word now only watched with a mixture of amusement and pity. He had spun a grand web, but in the end, he was the only one left tangled in it, while the truth—patient, steady, and ever-persistent—cleared the air like the first rains after a dry season.

Chapter Sixteen

The Arms of the Law (Or, When Ignorance Stops Being Bliss)

As The Narcissist's web of lies unraveled, he found himself facing a force he had never respected but now couldn't ignore: the law. In Kenya, where word spreads faster than a boda-boda on a free road, news of his antics reached beyond whispers and was now part of everyone's lunchtime gossip. And The Songbird, tired of playing the unassuming victim, had decided to let the legal system do what it does best. This time, it wasn't just chai gossip or Mama Mboga's opinion; it was legal, backed by facts, paperwork, and the weight of the constitution.

For years, The Narcissist had strutted through life with the kind of arrogance usually reserved for those who believe they're untouchable. He had always dismissed the law as a mere inconvenience, something for "other people." The mere idea that he might face consequences seemed to him like a bad joke. But now, armed with the sharp mind of her no-nonsense lawyer, JL, and the spirit of the constitution, The Songbird decided it was time to remind him that charm and half-baked tales weren't substitutes for accountability.

The summons arrived like a wake-up call in the dead of the night. The Narcissist was shocked—actual documents, signed and stamped, made their way into his life. "Haiya!" he muttered, rereading the papers in disbelief. "Surely, they can't be serious? Me?" But there it was, in black and white, unmistakable and official. His only choice now was to face the reality he'd avoided for so long. The days of side-stepping responsibility were over, and his once-cocky attitude quickly deflated, transforming into a flurry of nervous excuses.

The Narcissist tried to maintain his usual bravado. At first, he shrugged it off, saying, "Mimi? Ati summons? Kwani what have I done?" to his dwindling crowd of supporters. But even they, once so ready to cheer on his tales, were now less enthusiastic, their loyalty having shriveled under the light of the truth. The papers in his hand weren't rumors or idle threats. They were the hard evidence of the law coming for him, not caring about his charm, his tall tales, or his habit of wriggling out of sticky situations.

With each legal document, his confidence waned. The papers reminded him of the boundaries he could no longer ignore—boundaries backed by the constitution and signed by officials who didn't care one bit for his charisma. Every carefully spun lie, every attempt to manipulate others, was collapsing under the weight of accountability. Gone were the days of captivating speeches at the local nyama choma joint; now, his words were stammered mutterings, his formerly grand stories reduced to weak excuses.

In one last, desperate attempt to save face, The Narcissist tried to rally his supporters. He called them up, recounted his revised stories, and tried to summon sympathy. But this time, there were no eager nods, no murmurs of agreement. His supporters had grown weary, the charm they once admired now appearing thin and hollow. The power he thought he held had, in reality, been nothing but air.

As he watched the crowd drift away, he realized the truth: his empire of lies had never been built on solid ground. It was merely a house of cards that had toppled the moment someone chose to stand up to him. For all his swagger, his charm, and his elaborate stories, he was left alone to face the law, which, unlike his tales, could not be swayed or ignored. In the end, the law was just as The Songbird knew it would be: steady, unwavering, and unbothered by anything less than the truth.

Chapter Seventeen

The Begging Begins (Or, How the Mighty Have Fallen)

When the walls of his well-built castle of deceit finally caved in, The Narcissist made a move so unexpected, it could've been straight from one of Kenya's favorite TV dramas. Gone was the strutting, loud-mouthed braggart who once commanded attention at every turn. He showed up before The Songbird, not with his usual arrogance, but in the most unexpected manner: begging. Yes, begging, as if his life depended on it.

The Songbird watched him approach, thoroughly bemused. She could barely believe this was the same person who had once slandered her to every boda rider and mama mboga from Westlands to Kibera. Here he was, trying to pull a complete 180, like a seasoned actor trying his luck in a role that was clearly out of his range.

"Oh, so now you want peace?" she said, arching an eyebrow in disbelief. "Hold on, let me call the press; surely, they'll want to capture this historic moment."

The Narcissist, visibly uncomfortable, squirmed as he searched for the right words. "Look, let's just call it even. I don't want any more trouble," he said, his voice barely above a whisper, as if he feared the walls themselves might mock him.

She chuckled, shaking her head with that kind of amusement you reserve for clueless children and stubborn goats. "You spent ages burning down the bridge," she reminded him, "then threw stones from the other side of the river. And now you show up, asking if we can pretend none of it happened?" She paused, letting the silence drive her point home. "That's a special kind of math, right there."

His mask, that smug confidence he wore like an oversized suit, started to crack under her words. He'd expected her to be the same soft-spoken woman he'd once known—the one he thought would forgive and forget. But instead, she stood firm, a pillar of quiet strength and wit. She'd spent enough time learning to stand her ground, and if he thought his charms would work on her now, he was more deluded than a Nairobi driver during rush hour.

He shifted nervously, looking down at his shoes as if they might offer him a way out. But even he could feel it: he wasn't facing just The Songbird. He was staring into the mirror of his own deeds, realizing, perhaps too late, the weight of his actions. She didn't have to say anything more; her calm gaze and subtle smile said it all.

And just like that, he gave one final sigh and slunk away, his shoulders drooping under the weight of defeat. He had come seeking a ceasefire but found himself facing the flames of his own making. As he disappeared from her life, his once-deafening presence faded into nothingness. In the end, the last thing he heard wasn't her forgiveness but the sound of her laughter, bright and free, ringing through the air as if to say, "I survived, and now I thrive."

Chapter Eighteen

Shaking the Things Without a Solid Foundation (Or, How Empires Made of Ego Always Crumble)

They say that nothing here on earth is permanent. Empires have come and gone, wealth is as fleeting as a Nairobi rainstorm, and health—well, that's about as predictable as the matatus. Yet somehow, we humans love to pretend otherwise, building our lives on flimsy foundations of pride, status, and the illusion that control is in our hands. The Narcissist, in his grandiosity, had tried just that, stacking up his shaky empire of half-truths, dramatics, and ego like a house of cards on a windy day.

But life has a way of shaking things up, especially when they're built on nonsense. The problem with foundations made of sand—and by "sand," I mean lies, manipulation, and a sense of superiority—is that they can't withstand the inevitable storms. They can't withstand the winds of change, the rains of reality, or the lightning strikes of accountability. And when those storms come, those without true substance find themselves ankle-deep in the mud, wondering why their castles have turned to rubble. And no, not even a prayer circle can rebuild what wasn't solid to begin with.

The Narcissist's empire was a perfect example. All his charm, his carefully crafted reputation, and his legion of "fans" couldn't save him from the storm of truth. He had tried to bend reality to his will, but reality, it turns out, is stubbornly resistant to lies. And the truth? Well, the truth is like a cockroach—no matter what you do, it somehow survives.

The Songbird and The Quiet One, in contrast, had learned that the only foundation worth building on is love. Real, inconvenient, sometimes unexplainable love. The kind that doesn't need labels or grand declarations, but that's always there, quiet and steady. It was love, after all, that had kept The Songbird standing strong through every false accusation, every whispered rumor, and every time The Narcissist had tried to shake her spirit. It was the quiet, resilient kind of love that had no ego, no conditions, and no pretense. And no amount of slander could tear that down.

Because here's the thing: pride-driven adventures may look impressive for a time, but they're about as safe as building on quicksand. And while lies may offer a temporary refuge, they're nothing more than flimsy shelters that crumble under the weight of reality. But love? Real love? It's like a house built on rock, able to withstand even the fiercest storms, because it's not dependent on appearances, opinions, or ego.

In the end, The Narcissist's empire of ego faded like a mirage. His lies disintegrated, his audience moved on, and the world didn't stop spinning. And there, standing quietly amidst the rubble, were The Songbird and The Quiet One, unshaken and unchanged. For while pride and pretense are fragile, love—genuine love—proves time and again to be the only thing with a foundation that can stand against whatever life decides to throw.

So, as the dust settled and life moved on, there was one lesson that stood tall amidst the ruins: when you build with love, not even the fiercest winds can take it down. And maybe, just maybe, that's the only empire worth building.

Appendix
Poems of Love, Battle, and Victory

1. The Symphony of Us

In Nairobi's chaos, where matatus honk,
A songbird's voice makes traffic stop and gawk.
"Is that a serenade or a cat in a fight?"
"Oh wait, it's just me, singing with all my might!"
With a quiet companion who'd rather not speak,
Their bond was a puzzle, delightfully unique.
While others looked puzzled, scratching their heads,
They were crafting a love story, laughing instead.

2. The Dance of Drama

Life's a stage, and oh, what a show!
With a narcissist casting a shadowy glow.
"Assassination plots?" he cried with a flair,
While The Songbird and Quiet One just giggled and stared.
"Next, he'll claim I'm a spy or a rogue in disguise!"
Said the Quiet One, rolling his eyes.
"Let him play villain, it's all in good fun,
We'll turn his grand drama into a pun!"

3. The Mystery of Love

What is this bond, so strange and absurd?
Is it love, friendship, or something unheard?
Some think it's an oddity, a circus of sorts,
But we know it's magic, with no need for reports.
In a world full of labels and needs to define,

We're just two quirky souls sipping sweet wine.
While they ponder and speculate, we simply roll on,
In the riddle of love, we're the perfect con.

4. The Battle Won

With whispers and gossip like bees in a hive,
The narcissist's lies were buzzing alive.
But with humor as armor and laughter our shield,
We laughed in his face, refusing to yield.
"Take your best shot!" the Songbird would cheer,
"Your lies are like confetti, they just disappear!"
And when all was said, when the smoke cleared away,
Love was the victor, come what may!

5. The Victory of Laughter

When life throws you curveballs and drama galore,
Why sulk in despair when you can just snore?
For every wild rumor, a punchline awaits,
And laughter's the ticket to opening gates.
"Did you hear the latest?" the Quiet One grinned,
"Turns out I'm a wizard! Who would have pinned?"
With chuckles and giggles, they spun through the strife,
Making memories brighter, adding joy to their life.

6. The Endless Journey

Years may go by, and wrinkles may sprout,
But our love's still a dance, without any doubt.

We don't need an ending, or a finale that's neat,
Just a lifetime of laughter and adventures to greet.
So here's to the moments that make our hearts sing,
To silly inside jokes and the joy that they bring.
In the mystery of us, let's raise a toast high,
For the greatest love story is the one that can fly!

About the Authors

The Co-Conspirators of Laughter and Love

In the bustling world of storytelling, two dynamic authors have banded together to create a whimsical universe filled with love, laughter, and the occasional melodramatic narcissist. They are passionate about penning tales that dance on the fine line between reality and absurdity, leaving readers both chuckling and pondering the mysteries of the heart.

Author 1: The Dreamy Wordsmith

Meet the Dreamy Wordsmith, a gospel singer by day and a master of romantic prose by night. With a voice that can melt ice caps and lyrics that resonate like a heartbeat, she weaves tales that draw on her musical background, infusing her stories with rhythm and soul. When she's not serenading the world, she can be found dodging the paparazzi (or maybe just her cat) while concocting plots thicker than her grandmother's ugali.

With a knack for turning mundane moments into hilarious anecdotes, she believes that laughter is the best ingredient in any love story. Her mission? To show the world that true love can be found even in the chaos of Nairobi traffic (or at least in a matatu with good Wi-Fi).

Author 2: The Quirky Scribe

And then there's the Quirky Scribe, who, like a stealthy ninja, emerges from the shadows armed with a laptop and a cup of coffee strong enough to power a small village. Known for his dry wit and sardonic humor, he crafts narratives that will leave you laughing, crying, and questioning your life choices—all in the span of a single chapter.

While he often prefers the company of his books to that of actual people, he excels in capturing the nuances of human relationships, especially the complex dynamics of love and friendship. He firmly believes that every good story needs a sprinkle of absurdity, and he's here to deliver that in spades. Rumor has it that his guilty pleasure is binge-watching soap operas to fuel his inspiration for outrageous plot twists.

Together, They Create Magic

Together, these two authors bring an unbeatable combination of lyrical artistry and sharp humor. Their partnership is a testament to the rare bonds they write about: a blend of mutual respect, friendship, and a shared love for life's ridiculousness.

When not crafting stories, you can find them arguing over the best matatu routes, planning their next literary heist, or just sharing a laugh over a cup of chai (or, let's be real, an entire pot). They invite you to join them on this wild ride through their imaginative tales, where every chapter promises to be as delightful as a matatu ride during rush hour—full of surprises, a few bumps, and endless joy.

Did you love *Love Beyond Time A Comedy of Divine Connection*? Then you should read *Hope and Healing: A Chaplain's Handbook*[1] by Kayumba David!

[2]

As a survivor of a challenging illness, I have experienced firsthand the profound impact that compassionate care can have on individuals in their most vulnerable moments. My journey through a robust healthcare environment in Belgium illuminated the critical role that various professionals play in the healing process. Nurses, doctors, and countless other healthcare staff dedicate themselves to the well-being of their patients, often going above and beyond to ensure that each person feels valued

1. https://books2read.com/u/mg6dYX

2. https://books2read.com/u/mg6dYX

and cared for. Their unwavering commitment to service inspires not only hope but also a sense of dignity during difficult times.

In writing this book, I am compelled to reflect on the significant contributions of those who serve in hospitals and other care settings, particularly chaplains who offer spiritual guidance and emotional support. They are the quiet yet powerful voices that provide comfort, instilling hope where despair often threatens to take root. Chaplains walk alongside patients and families, navigating the challenges of illness, suffering, and the uncertainty of life and death.

This guide aims to illuminate the path of chaplaincy in various environments, particularly within hospitals and prisons. It is a call to those who feel the tug of a sacred vocation, encouraging them to embrace their role as vessels of God's love and grace. It is my hope that this book serves as a source of inspiration and practical guidance for current and future chaplains, empowering them to foster healing, reconciliation, and transformation in the lives of those they serve.

May this work resonate with anyone who seeks to understand the beauty and importance of compassionate ministry, reminding us all of the profound difference that care and hope can make in our world.

Read more at www.zcews.org.